Cigar Box Stories

Cigar Box Stories

Cigar Box Stories

By

John Allen Boyd

R.C. Linnell Publishing

Cigar Box Stories

Cover design by Dave Davis

ISBN – 13: 978-0-9840025-4-2
ISBN – 10: 09840025-4-5

Published by
R. C. Linnell Publishing
Louisville, KY 40205
www.LinnellPublishing.com

Other publications by John Allen Boyd:
Sunbonnets and Sweet Gum (ISBN: 1-4010-3406-3)
Emerson Avery, That Latin Teacher (ISBN: 978-1-4415-1648-0)

Contact him:
johnallenboyd@gmail.com

ACKNOWLEDGMENTS

iii

First and foremost I wish to thank Cheri Powell of R. C. Linnell Publishing for her knowledge and skills in nurturing this book to publication. Also, much gratitude to my friends in the Friday Writer's Group at The Reader's Corner in Louisville: Beverly Giammara, Heidi Saunders, Susan Treitz, K Shaver, Maggie Riley, Bryant Stamford, Deanna O'Daniel, Mary Ann Fitzharris, David Owen, Steve Hall, Heather Thomas, Ed Koffenberger, and Leslie Moise. Also to Mary Popham. Special thanks to John Wayne Taylor who listens and advises.

PREFACE

This collection of short stories, poetry, and articles is for those who find interest in folklore and creative writing expressed through fascinating characters. In my mind it is held together by a few words of Tennyson, from his extended poem, *Ulysses*: "*...I am a part of all that I have met...*" To me this is a philosophic stance that accompanies me daily as I deal with people, friends and strangers alike. I think nothing in life is self-contained and that, truly, when any two people interact they exchange some of each to each. Looking back over my lifetime, I am populated by vast numbers of people whom I grew up with, went to colleges with, spent time in the Army and in my classrooms with. In writing the contents of this book, I have recalled a mere handful of people, most more fictional than real.

For a number of years, I taught in rural areas of Kentucky and loved it in spite of insufficient pay. While in Nelson County and Warren County, I soaked up their dialects and cultures, and I kept a careful eye out for the local characters. A fascinating venture for me.

There are a variety of writings herein, even a ghost story plunked down along with the stories from rural Kentucky. At the end of the book are three articles that are not fiction - about two of my favorite people and about my surrogate family.

If you wish, please contact me with your comments after reading this book.

Wishing you well,

John Allen Boyd
Louisville, KY
June, 2012
johnallenboyd@gmail.com

Table of Contents

Kentucky Bachelor Farmer
Page 3

Farmboy
Page 17

A Little No-Name Story
Page 19

Knife
Page 25

The Phone Call
Page 27

Hunched-Up Woman
Page 31

Sons and Fathers
Page 33

Lobo
Page 41

Dead Child with Open Eyes
Page 43

Ethan Talbot Carney
Page 51

A Folk Tale in Threes
Page 57

Big Muncey
Page 63

A Country Passing
Page 73

Intimacy and the Token
Page 77

Survival
Page 83

Uncle Elmon
Page 85

Eugene
Page 95

Little Imp
Page 107

Old Emmett
Page 109

The Hazards of Reading
Page 117

Yea, Though I Walk
Page 119

Amber, Wife and Mother
Page 125

Absolution
Page 129

Essy Barnett
Page 131

First Kiss
Page 139

Identity
Page 147

Sensitivity
Page 149

Summation
Page 155

The Faux War
Page 157

Interlude on the Bay
Page 165

Trappers on Return
Page 169

Dr. Gordon Wilson – How I remember Him*
Page 171

Some Thoughts About Our Music Teacher*
Page 183

The Fourth of July 2011*
Page 189

Fat Ass
Page 197

An Afterward
Page 201

*The three articles mentioned in the preface

Cigar
Box
Stories

Kentucky Bachelor Farmer

The first short story in the book - is it the best? One of the better, perhaps. It is linear fiction with a single point of view, mostly.

The young struggle
and they yearn for the time
when looking up
becomes looking across
now as equals
with histories
of their own

Kentucky Bachelor Farmer

Earl is the sort of man who would stay on at the home place for life, at the farm where he grew up. And he could never think otherwise.

 The way he tells it, "My other brothers and sisters moved on down the road over to Bowling Green and Nashville. They wanted more than our home place could offer. Too lonely an' cut off for them all in spite of our sweet memories and good times. So I stayed on with Mom and Pop, and we got letters full of homesick now and then. Pretty much had to run the place by myself. Quiet days and nights, but it suits me here. Then my baby sister, Myra, come back. She didn't have no place to go when her husband got sent off to fight in Korea. So she brung little Bunky and them two pint-sized girls here. Jest fine with me. Livened up the place. Then her husband done got killed the first year he was over there. And Mom died a year after Pop - just before Kennedy was elected. You know how it is. People in families dies in threes. I got their pictures sittin' on the fire-board. So I was glad Myra come back home. I needed someone to help out, and the kitchen just wasn't the same without Mom.

 "Them lil'l uns of Myra! Law! They shore was a hand-full when they was still chil-ren. After he got old enough to help out with chores, I musta worked that boy Bunky pretty hard 'cause he took off 'bout the time he hit seventeen. Went an' joined up in the Army. Left us a note on the table, and we ain't heard much from him since. Worries Myra half sick with Viet Nam still going on and all. But we keep at it here and doin' right well. Myra and the girls tend to washin' dirty clothes and the cannin' and cookin'. Even hep out with the chores.

 "She keeps a pretty close eye on them girls of her'n, but I been seein' guys comin' by more 'n more often. Both of them gals out of school now. Always lots of doings and noises around the place with them living here. Talkin' a lot about startin' they own families. And that sister of mine, Myra. She been talkin' a right smart to Billy Ray Cozine in town of late."

So, Earl stayed home and became a bachelor farmer out at the old Caudill place not far from town. Lanky, muscular, friendly as a puppy. Even tempered and a hard working farmer. His life and the life of the farm merged into one.

The town: New Briar, Kentucky. Little hamlet with one blinking light where the two state roads intersect. Population at last count was down to 412. At one time, back in its heyday before the interstate system, the population stayed around 800 for over a hundred years. A steady stream of traffic rumbling through. Business in town remained stable. But not much commerce these days. Typically local folks. Since I-65 opened and the little high schools consolidated into one big school over toward E-town, most of the younger generation have been moving away for better jobs or college, and they only come back for special occasions. That, and with the old folks dying off, New Briar itself is almost dead. Many active farms that lasted for generations sit idle, and some have become family retreats. Silos crumbling and covered with vines. Here and there tobacco barns tilting with big doors and side vents missing - rusted roofing peeled back in spots. However, a scattering of working farms remains. Farmers loyal to their families and tradition continue raising cattle, pigs, tobacco, corn, soy beans, horses - whatever to survive and cling to their way of life. Just like Earl Caudill.

The Caudill farm is out on Gooseneck Creek Road. Earl and those other remaining farmers continue to honor the customs and ways of that part of Kentucky, of the land of their births out a ways from New Briar. They never tire of living there, of taking a private inventory of the lay of its land

and its beauty through each season, of knowing every turn of the road and each landmark by name.

Then, one ordinary afternoon, Bunky came home. Myra's son. Earl's nephew. He left still a skinny teenager and now has walked into the house a twenty-four year old man home from Viet Nam. When Myra focused on the soldier in uniform standing in the doorway and recognized him as her son, she let out a squawk and rushed to him, hugged him, and kissed his cheek. He lit up, embarrassed, and became swept up with the tenderness of his return to his mom and the home place. Then, mumbling, she immediately began rushing about in the kitchen preparing food she remembered that Bunky liked best: fried chicken, mashed potatoes, green beans, and drop biscuits.

His sisters stared at Bunky in wonder, unsure of this grown man who used to tease and pick on them. Turning to them, awkwardly, he opened his arms, and they both rushed into his embrace with hugs and squeals, sniffing him in hopes of recollecting his scent. His eyes roamed as he inventoried the contents of the room: the table, chairs, pot-bellied stove, that old picture of the shepherds praying, the vase of his grandmother, and, especially, the sisters and how they had grown up and changed.

Coming to the house from the barn, Earl heard the commotion. He opened the side door and saw a soldier. A man his size. The scene of a uniformed man, the girls squealing, and Myra rushing about in the kitchen all came together in his mind. His nephew had come back. That boy Bunky had returned. Must be seven years now and hardly a word from him. Earl turned and made long strides toward Bunky. In the awkwardness of two men greeting each other, Bunky, timidly and formally, reached out for a handshake. But Earl ignored it and did something he would never ordinarily do. He pulled his nephew to him and hugged him in close, aware of the cool skin of Bunky's ear to his cheek. Both of them pulled with their arms and felt the hands of the other patting at their backs. Bunky had come home.

Word traveled fast. Before dark, everyone in and around town knew that Bunky, the Caudill boy who had run off at seventeen, had made it back. A few of Myra's friends, mothers of other boys gone off to war, phoned and spoke obliquely about Bunky's return, carefully inquiring to see if he had been wounded or was shell-shocked. His excited sisters stayed busy answering the telephone and calling out. And three mothers of sons killed in Viet Nam dropped by together to savor Myra's joy and re-live their lost dreams. Only one lost it and wept. They didn't stay long.

Several friends of Bunky's sisters also called to find out about him - if he were married to a Japanese girl or hung up on drugs. Secret schemes and plots for introductions and dates were already being hatched in the heads of his sisters and their friends. And while his mother was full of activity in the kitchen and with visitors and the phone, she stopped once, startled at the sudden intrusion of an idea: perhaps Bunky will marry a local girl and settle down and give her grandchildren. Sooner than later, she hoped.

Late, after ten that night, Earl went up to his room upstairs, The Boys' Room, across the hall from The Girls' Room. It occurred to him that he would be sharing the room with Bunky, so Earl fixed the other bed for him. Clean sheets, pillow case, and the light quilt from the trunk at the foot of his own bed. Later, hearing movement in his bedroom, he opened an eye to watch Bunky quietly stripping down to his shorts and slipping under the bed-covers with no more sound than the whispers of skin on fresh white sheets. Then there was no sound beyond a long, low exhalation from Bunky.

The next day, Earl lifted back his covers and swiveled his legs over to the side of his bed and peered at the shape of Bunky face down deep in sleep on the other side of his room.

Listening to the even breathing of Bunky, Earl dressed soundlessly and padded down the stairs. He put on his boots sitting at the table and breathed in the different smells in the house - the remnants of cigarette smoke and perfumes and powders remaining from the visitors. And there was that other thing, the aura of an additional man in the house. He left through the back door to do the morning chores. "I'll let him sleep late today," Earl whispered aloud as he stepped into the fresh, cool morning.

Even after the sun was fully up, his mother and sisters tip-toed around the old farm house so as not to waken Bunky. Around noon they heard him poking about upstairs in Earl's room. He was hunting for blue jeans and a flannel shirt in Earl's dresser. Bunky wondered if he just might fit into Earl's clothes - if he had grown into the size of his uncle.

Soon he appeared in the kitchen dressed in his Army boots and Earl's work clothes. He knew it was a good fit. The girls remarked about his muscles, and they poked at his stomach and squeezed his biceps with admiration. His mother fed him a late breakfast which he devoured while his sisters sat at the table with him and watched him work through a slab of country ham, three eggs over easy, drop-biscuits with homemade blackberry jam, cold white milk, and two cups of coffee with extra sugar and cream. Real cream. He could not keep up with their questions and comments. Inevitably, someone asked about what it was like in Viet Nam. Myra paused and lifted her head and the girls raised their eyebrows when they heard his voice rise a slight bit and blurt out, "I ain't gonna ever talk about that stuff. Never." The girls and Myra saw the change of his face, the different placement of his eyebrows, the sudden hurt in his eyes, and they understood. After he ate the last biscuit, he leaned back and lit a cigarette. He stretched his long arms out to the side and up over his head, the cords of muscles at his neck popping up. He grinned at them and stated evenly, "Coffee and a cigarette. And home."

Earl came lumbering in from the back field where he had spent the morning cultivating the young tobacco plants with his red Farmall tractor, his pride and joy. In the instant that he scanned the room and had surveyed his family and had taken in the smells of breakfast and Bunky's cigarette, Earl assessed Bunky's mood. His nephew was luxuriating in having reached his dream of safety and home and of being fawned over by his mother and sisters. Earl imagined, just guessing, that this must have been his reverie for years - as he lay in foxholes and trenches with explosions around him and bullets buzzing over his head and into the dirt nearby - as he attempted to wash the stench of rotted human flesh from his boots after he had stepped into a corpse while he was running in the dark - as he struggled to maintain his sanity in the company of soldiers on other missions - as he wrestled with knowing he was anonymous, just a GI, an orphan without his family. Earl pulled into his mind the great relief his nephew must be experiencing this clear bright day back home at long last.

Smiling, Earl took his usual seat at the head of the table. He had plans for Bunky that day and asked him, "You gonna hang around here for a few days, ain't cha, Bunky?"

The girls looked at Bunky hopefully. Myra was listening intently in the kitchen.

Bunky lifted his chin and eyebrows. "Probably," he replied. Then, reacting to the quick looks of apprehension on their faces, he said, "Yes."

Earl, careful that his words placed the two of them on an equal man-to-man basis, said, "When you finished there, let's me and you go out and look over the farm. Get you outta the house. Maybe drive 'round a bit and see things."

Again, Bunky lifted his chin and eyebrows in acceptance. Within moments, he and Earl were out of the house. His sisters and mother crowding at the side door watching them drive off on the tractor, Earl driving and Bunky standing off balance on the small running board, leaning back onto the fender next to his uncle.

Earl took Bunky on the grand tour of the farm, to the tobacco field, the pond, the garden, and to the ancient milk barn. At each place, the two of them climbed down for a look. Earl was careful to walk side-by-side with Bunky and never to lead him or treat him with the slightest hint of indifference. By the time they had parked the Farmall in the shed and walked to the truck, Bunky had picked up on his new importance to Earl. No longer would his uncle treat him as a kid. He realized that the signals from Earl placed them as equals on the family farm and probably in life. It became clear to Bunky that Earl wanted him to stay and be a partner on the family farm. After the years he spent in the Army, the idea was settling comfortably in his mind.

It was along toward late afternoon, an hour or so before farmers had to do their late milking, when they drove off in the truck, to the only beer joint in New Briar. It was a white cinderblock place at the edge of town - the first building on arriving in town. Since it was owned and operated by Bob Satterly, everyone called it "Bob's Place." Bob and his family lived next door. No sign hung over the entrance, though there was a small electric beer advertisement in the little window next to the door. Trucks and a few cars were already parked out front on the rough gravel surface. Behind Bob's Place, out of sight from the road, there would, no doubt, be a truck or two where owners parked them to make it difficult for wives or other stalkers to find them.

Earl pulled in to a space out front between two pickups and laughed as if at something he was remembering. Bunky waited for his uncle to tell him. As though the two of them were trusted friends who could share gossip and secrets, Earl chortled and said, "While you gone, Bob's roof blowed off."

"Roof blowed off? Looks same to me."

"Well, John Robert was driving by on his way to church of a Sunday morning, an' just as he got next to Bob's Place there was the damndest boom. He said one end of the roof, the end right over the kitchen part, just lifted up in the air and dropped back down in place. All the winders was blowed out. He said 'fore he got stopped that Bob was already runnin' outter his house scared to death. His wife, Betty - you 'member - she cooked chili and hamburgers in there and too dumb to work the cash register - she'd done left a turned-off gas burner just barely on, and when the gas reached up to the pilot, kaboom!"

Bunky snorted in laughter and grinned. His eyes sparkled. He felt some elation at coming here and listening to Earl talk to him so comfortably. Before, he had never been old enough to enter Bob's Place. It had always been there on the side of the road just at the edge of "The Brar" (as he and his buddies called the little town), but he had never been in it, in that place of grown men, big men, a dark place of secrets that men kept from the ears of kids. And now, here he was. About to go into Bob's Place as a man. He imagined that groups of men would be seated and nursing their beers. That they would turn and look up at him and see him differently now.

Bunky climbed out of the truck and checked his posture making himself stand tall and walk tall. He was ready to pass in a different type of review than in the army.

As they stepped inside the little beer joint, every man looked openly at them. Three men immediately stood and, one by one, walked over with his hand extended to Bunky. They had been in the Korean War. Veterans themselves. Word had reached them that a fellow warrior had returned from this new, different war. They recognized the soldier part of each other instantly, and the men welcomed Bunky into this place of safety where men could talk and relax together. As they greeted him and clasped hands, they looked knowingly and directly into each others' eyes. In every instance, an unexplainable energy, perhaps a knowledge, was exchanged. Each of them was committed to passing over the horrors and killing in silence.

Earl led Bunky to the bar stools and kept back allowing Bunky to soak up the feeling of the place and the ways of the men in it, inviting him to join him and the other men. And Bunky felt welcomed here. Without doubt, he was their equal now. He was a Caudill returned home to the old Caudill place out on Gooseneck Creek Road. Maybe come home to stay.

There was a juke-box in the corner - Hank Williams, "Your Cheatin' Heart." It suited the place, its dim lights and smoke, the stale tang of beer and sweat, a few glitters from beer signs. Bob had two bare electric lights hanging from the low ceiling over the main part of the bar room, each with a white enameled plate-sized reflector. A thin haze of smoke added to the dimness of the place. Earl guided Bunky to the bar, and Bunky turned to face the room, his elbows behind him resting on the bar - striking a pose, Earl thought. Bunky studied the place.

Brown. Inside it was a brown place of brown unvarnished wood, even the walls and floor, the tables and chairs, the six bar stools, all various shades of brown. However, Bob kept the top of the bar counter itself somewhat shiny with constant swabbing. Unlike the muscular farmers, Bob had gone to fat, a friendly man with a quiet fatherly voice under a slick head. Most of the farmers in the room looked and dressed pretty much the same. Blue jeans, an occasional ten gallon hat, boots, flannel shirts or tee-shirts. Their hands were rough with coarse fingers, and they had strong, muscular arms and thick thighs. The size of their shoulders and rear-ends bespoke their ability to lift and carry. Their eyes moved carefully, fully opened and unafraid. They sat two or three to a table. One man sat alone on a stool at the end of the bar counter.

Under the sad and broken singing of Hank, the men settled back into slowly drinking their beers and talking to each other with occasional laughter. Bunky listened to the others - picking out threads of conversations. Two men were trying to outdo each other bemoaning their lack of pussy at home. "My old lady gonna bleed to death if she on the rag as much as she say she is." The man at the table with that one said, "I know just what you mean. I try and try to get mine in the mood. Got some of them pictures of women going at it with each other, and I give 'em to her hoping to start her motor. No way. Wouldn't even get me off any other ways nohows." Both of the men had hang-dog faces and were shaking their heads in rejection and commiseration.

At another table two younger men were sitting up straight and trading insults. "You been spending' lots a time in the barn lately. You ain't gittin' 'nough from Carla?"

"Yeah, well you won't find no stump-broke heifers in my barn grinning an' winking at me like I seen in yours last week."

His companion, stretching back, laughed and retorted, "Maybe you need to drive on down the road an' pay a visit to ol' Leon. I hear if you close your eyes you won't know the dif- fernce. All pink on the insides."

Both the men hooted at this and firmly shook their heads no.

Hank was singing "Tears in my Beer." At another table one man leaned close to the two other men with him. The man was very serious, and the other two watched his face but allowed their eyes to stray to other parts of the room now and then. He was telling them, "...says I don't understand her. Wants me to change my ways. What ways? I'm just me. Ain't nothing' I'm doing to hurt her. I give her money to buy clothes with. And we went out to a movie in Bowling Green just before Christmas. She hates it when I go hunting with you all. An when she fount out I went to that burlesque bar in

Nashville, all hell broke loose. It's got so I have to jack off three times a day. But I think a man's got the right..." On and on crying in his beer. The other two sitting there helpless.

Bunky was enjoying listening to the men in Bob's Place. He knew men often talk together with no holding back. Especially close friends. Bob, rubbing off a ring of wet on the bar, came over to him and said, "You can hear anything in here, Bunky. Most of it's just talk. Lettin' off steam."

The man at the end of the counter stood up and came up next to Bunky. Bob, behind the bar, grinned expectantly. Some of the others stopped talking and looked toward the bar. Bunky vaguely recognized the other man. J. O., who worked at the Standard station. He and J. O. shook hands. Firm strong grips. Then J. O. leaned back on the bar next to Bunky and said, "See that mark on the bar there?" He pointed to a notch in the bar about eight inches from the edge. A cut there. He said, "Betcha a beer the tip of my dick's long enough to touch that mark - me just up tight to the bar."

Bunky jerked his head back in surprise at that sort of talk. In the army he had witnessed all sorts of crudeness and fun among his buddies, but never from grown men in New Briar. That sort of talk was kept away from the younger boys. A few wild stories had circulated from time to time, but most of his buddies back then were more interested in their own lives and not the lives of older people. And here was a man Earl's age, in his forties, talking about the size of his dick. What did he care about J. O.'s dick? Jeez!

Bunky replied, "What?!"

"You heard me. If I can belly up to this bar and flop my limp dick out and the end of it touches that mark, you buy me a beer."

By then every man in the room was grinning. Some were scooting their chairs back and standing up to come over and watch. Obviously this had been done before to other people. Maybe many times. Bunky was not sure what to do and looked at Earl's face. Earl sat not moving with a slight smile on his face and making no motions to leave or to pop J. O. in the mouth. Bunky had a slight inkling that he was about to go through some sort of initiation ritual. Now every man in the room had crowded around them. Bob had stepped back and was grinning broadly, bobbing his head and half-snorting with laughter. One front tooth missing. The others gray and decayed.

Again Bunky looked at Earl who widened his eyes as if to say, "You're on your own." He could hear the men snickering. Bunky took all of this in and said, "All right, J. O. But I don't think you're man enough to win that beer."

J. O. smirked, looked at Bob, and said, "Get that cold brew ready, Bob. And here we go!" J. O. unzipped, reached in, and hauled out his penis, a truly monumental one. He mumbled, "Lemme just pull the hide back." He leaned up to the edge of the bar and unfolded it across the bar up to the notch and a bit beyond. Every man stared and either whistled or hooted. In an even voice Earl said, "Pay Bob for the beer, Bunky."

J. O. had won another bet. Nonchalantly he replaced his penis, zipped up, and took his beer back to the far stool. Bob turned toward the counter at the back wall with the mirror. Most of the men looked up at a thin metal rod extending from one end of the counter to the other, about twelve feet. On the left end of the rod were spring loaded clothes pins hanging down, one next to the other, each snapped onto the rod. Many of them. And each one had a name scrawled across the flat side. Bob opened a drawer and took out a new clothes pin, wrote "Bunky" on it and snapped it next to the last one on the rod. Bob counted the clothes pins out loud as the men waited. At thirty-nine, Earl laughed, "That's my number!"

At fifty-two one of the Korean veterans shouted out, "That's me!"

At sixty-nine another man ducked his head and the others pounded his back squawking with laughter. Bob reached the last clothes pin, Bunky's, and announced, "Well, Gents, that makes seventy-six." The room burst into laughter and good humor. Five men came up to Bunky and shook his hand. Each one told him which number he had been. Bunky joined in with their game reminding himself to remember his number. Seventy-six. J. O. was back on his stool sipping at his fresh beer nodding his head, the only man in the room without a number.

Within minutes, the men had settled back to their earlier places and were talking quietly. Earl nudged Bunky and leaned close to his ear saying, "See that man over there with the bald head?" Bunky looked in the mirror below the clothes pins and picked out the bald-headed man. Jimmy Avery it was. Earl spoke in a voice below the level of conversations and the nasal complaints of Hank on the juke box. "While you was gone, that man's daddy burned up. Really did! Burned up! While Jimmy and his wife and kids was at church one Sunday and then went on to shop in Bowling Green, the old man musta had a heart attack or something and he fallen into the fireplace. His body caught afire just like a piece of meat burning in its own grease. They come back and smelt that stinch of burnt meat 'fore they got in the door. Fount Old Man Avery's legs and butt sticking out of the fireplace on the floor and his upper half done burnt down to almost nothing."

Looking around, Bunky thought, What kind of story do they tell about Uncle Earl? And if I settle back home, what will my story be?

Farmboy

When do words become poetry? These days, I have no idea. Over the years as a teacher I have been sensitive to the plight of rural boys and girls who have little contact with their peer group except in school. Their daily isolation and missing feed-back from others as they attempt to develop a self-image. But for that matter, I think it is a universal endeavor.

Can there be a difference
between being a country boy
and a city or town boy
while seeking identity
in a mirror

Farmboy

He stood there
in the back part of the old farmhouse
and searched his face
confronting the substance of self
reaching back to him
from the blotted mirror
above the water bucket
and tin dipper

His solemn eyes
and moving hurt
enacted
by his brows and lips

When will I become a real person

Who will I be

Why am I alone

A Little No-Name Story

A linear short story, fiction, with a first person point of view about the ceremony of leaving home, going off to college. I admit to recalling a poignant painting by Normal Rockwell of a boy ready to leave the nest, waiting for a bus with his farmer dad .

Watching from a safe place
reaching out
one sees others as self
and can sing along
with their joys
their arrivals and departures
and those moments before each

A Little No-Name Story

I was loafing, just woolgathering inside the gas station in my tiny, dusty hometown and, through the window behind the cash register, I noticed this touching drama unfolding. A scene surprisingly like one of those poignant pictures painted by Norman Rockwell. A shiny-faced farm boy waiting for the bus at the edge of the highway - sitting on the running board of a weary farm truck next to his work-beaten old man - a cardboard suitcase off to his side and his dog at his knees. The boy's head high and alert, feet in new brown shoes and flat to the ground. Hands clasped together. Eyes wide open and eyebrows high.

His father was just the opposite. Ragged hands loose. Legs apart. Leaning forward and a little towards his son. His work hat pushed back revealing the demarcation between the tanned part of his face and the white skin above. Bib overalls. Boots that had a history of stepping in cow and pig manure. His face drawn and taut. I knew him to be a quiet man, and, indeed, he was not speaking. Seemed stymied and unable to conjure up any simple words. The picture of awkwardness waiting for the bus and the departure of his son. Only a few old-man sounds coming from him - the taking in of air through his nose and an occasional tongue noise and swallow.

The two of them, their minds circling around each other.

Even this morning, I imagined, while they were doing chores, he had rehearsed a few things to tell his boy. But they must have fled from him. High words for his son. A father's tributes and careful words of advice, perhaps. A scattering of admonitions. Maybe even halting, rare words of affection.

Standing at the window of the gas station, I recognized

the family drama unfolding just a few feet away. My own going away was about the same. Only I was going off to war and not to college.

The routines of farm life and chores linger imbedded in my own history, so I knew, even this morning, they had toiled without speaking during the routine morning milking, collection of eggs, and seeing to the dogs. There was a moment, I imagined, when the old man turned from slopping the hogs and peered through the morning haze at his son, watching him bringing buckets of well water to the house. I figured it took some effort for him to put away the images of his son as a child, and, instead, admit that he was now fully grown and broad shouldered.

After the bus arrives and the boy is off to college, I'll walk up to Jim's Git-Cha Some Bar and drink a beer with the old man. Listen to him tell about his boy. *I could always count on him. Work. That's what life's like on a farm. Ya know yerself how hit were fer you. All work all day. Sometimes relax a bit after supper. An' jest last night, in the light of the lantern while them dogs was running the scent of a coon, I looked him over a right smart while we listened for the dogs. Hit was my boy's face and eyes in the lantern light. The way they was shining with excitement. Glittering so. Then ole Annie Dog's high barks a-chopping at that treed coon. Her head up singing to us. I jest caint speak of it.*

The boy's head popped up in a jerk when he caught sight of the bus - before the old man did. It rumbled up to the side of the filling station, the high reverberations of it lowering to a tame roar as it settled into idling. The door hissed as it swung open, and, during this undoing, I noticed the farmer stiffen, as if suddenly he felt something coming loose inside himself in the urgency of the moment that seemed to swallow him.

Next to the boy's leg, his dog, Pup, looked concerned. Confused. It was an occasion the dog had not encountered, along with the different smells from the boy. Fresh clothes, hair oil, and after shave.

The old man got up and peered through the door, into the interior of the bus, into the dark cave there. But the boy looked into the door and saw colors, chrome, and a dashboard with dials and instruments in front of the oversized steering wheel. Behind him he heard the whine of concern from Pup and turned, knelt down, and gave it a rub and a hug. A nervous, asking whine and tentative wag of its tail. Standing next to the boy, the old man was slowly shifting his weight from side to side to get the kinks out from sitting too long.

The bus driver was jolly. I recognized him. Fresh out of the Army. Home from the war and glad of it. "Let's have your ticket, young man, or do I need to issue you one?" The old farmer tried for a reply, one grown man to the other, but his words got stuck. So the boy spoke out. "To Bowling Green, sir. One way."

The driver looked at the farmer and the dog and saw it all. To me, watching, he was remembering his own going away to boot camp. That indelible image caught forever in his mind's eye. *Off to the Army to fight the Nazis or Japs. For home and country. My duty. Mom and Pop - and little sister there squeezing her rag doll. And my best friend, Cousin Jake, too young to go. That blazing morning sun. Each of them forcing a smile just for me. To take with me. With their backs straight and chests out. With pride. Probably fearful and not wanting to show it.*

The driver looked at the boy and said, "That'll be precisely one dollar and thirteen cents cash money, young man." The farmer flipped his cigarette, watched it descend, and stubbed it with his boot. Reached into his bib pocket and wrangled out his change purse, soft leather with a bronze snap. He dug out the coins and counted them, one by one, into the driver's hand. A half dollar, a quarter, three dimes, and exactly eight pennies - each one warm from his chest. He fumbled the last penny, and the boy caught it before it hit the ground. Handed it to the driver while inspecting his bus uniform, no doubt wondering what he had done in the war. How many men he had killed.

The driver took the boy's suitcase and carried it to the side of the bus, opened a long panel and added it to the other bags and bundles there. A whistling man, the driver went into the gas station to get the key to the restroom. The bus idling. Diesel sounds and its sharp smells. Pup wagging its tail, looking from the boy to the old man. The boy's body jumpy with excitement. Pulsing as he stood waiting. The farmer's stance as still as a scarecrow. Neither one looking at the other. I figured the father was surely thinking of all the added work without his boy. The son, no doubt thinking of the world out there. The possibilities. The ideas. The people. Newness.

The driver returned and recognized the awkwardness of the moment. "Say goodbye to your daddy, youngster. Time to get a move on." For a split second, for a lifetime to me, the boy and father stood caught in the other's eyes. The old man tilted forward, almost the beginning of a stumble, regained his balance, and thrust out his hand. This is the part that always stops my breathing, when a father and son have the occasion to show each other their love. The boy saw the hand. Scanned the coarse wrinkles and freckles. He placed his hand there, and they pumped. Once. Twice. And let go. Both of them embarrassed. Perhaps wanting more. Fearing a hug - or a kiss, even.

The father took in a breath and forced out the words, "Watch your money. Write to your mother." That was all.

From inside the bus, the boy found a seat at the right so he could keep sight of his pop and his dog. At a window. The bus began. It was as if I were with him listening to the roaring and gears. His body weight shifting with the lunging of the bus. In the window the town moved, and he watched his father and his dog and the farm truck diminish and slip out of sight. His father squinting at the bus and nodding his head.

From inside the service station, I kept my eyes on Pup, his tail no longer wagging, looking up at the boy's pop and wondering about all of this.

Knife

High writing - is it poetry? This is about a young boy as he watches an old man whittling and caressing his knife. About the young learning from the old. The boy's yearning for a "grown-up knife."

Old men
amused
know they are being studied
by little boys
and put on a show
of manly arts

Knife

The old farmer
sitting most of his days
on the shaded bench in town
leans forward
and turns his treasure over
in wide hardened hands
a bone-handled pocket knife
the long blade opened and out

And I am a boy
fixed on watching
men
in performance
and I have already mastered spitting

He knows I am studying
how he opens and closes
the finely honed blades
and takes a showman's moment
to razor off a patch of hair from his forearm

With a quick swallow
eyebrows lifted
and tongue to upper lip
he ceremoniously snaps the long blade
to the half notch
and then to its nest
while leaning forward
over the curls of cedar around his feet
making his declaration
of manhood
to another young boy

The Phone Call

A linear, humorous phone dialogue between two former teachers. It is mostly fiction and certainly iconoclastic.

Some people
needing to talk
have forgotten
how to listen
or are they
just hoggish
by nature

The Phone Call

It is a sweet summer day. Not too hot. The sort of day with occasional cumulus clouds. I think of a little domed white marble structure, a pristine rotunda suitable for a Greek oracle. It would fit neatly across the field on the side of the hill. And a unicorn....

Braaaaing...branng.

Hello.

Well, Ronald, aren't you something not sending me a Christmas card and I sent you one from Paul and me. Debbie said you have had some health issues, and I've waited all these months to find out if you're still alive....

Evelyn? Is this Evelyn Blankenbaker?

Well, of course. Who else? I was just sitting here thinking about those programs from the BBC. You know. "Keeping Up Appearances" and "Last of the Summer Wine." I hope you watch them. I just love Thora Hird. I guess I should say, Dame Thora Hird even though her face looks like a baboon's butt. She plays Nora, that one the ugly man is always trying to kiss.

Well, actually, I looked her up on the internet, and Dame Hird plays the wife of the mechanic....

Oh, no. That can't be right. So how are you?

I'm all right. I had a quadruple bypa....

When I had my hemorrhoids removed, I've never had so much pain. And when time came to have a bowel movement, I wanted to die, the pain was so dreadful. And bloody. My god, what a mess.

When was that, Evel...?

Debbie said you've been writing a novel. What's it about?

About an old man who returns to his...

Now I want you to get me a copy of it when it comes out.

Ernie Spencer still hasn't got his book published. I read it and just loooved it. The best thing I ever read. When I had him in English class, I just knew he would be a great writer some day.

What was his book abo...?

Oh, you haven't read the manuscript? It's the best THING. I swear. The main character is a modern Jesus in a coal mine. It just makes me shiver.

Did Ernie try to find an agent?

He had his wife look for one, but the book is so good that she sent a copy of the manuscript to a publisher. Harper and Row, I think. But they sent it right back. No kiss my ass or nothing. Those publishing companies just want sex and violence, you know. Nothing good. I want you to tell him how to go about getting it published.

Well, several years ago his wife called me about how to self-publish....

Tell me about your surgery. So help me, if I ever get hemorrhoids again I think I'd just tell them to knock me in the head.

I was weak for...

Did you go to Teddy Kellog's wake over at Beuford's funeral... I mean Lewis's funeral home. I keep thinking of it as Beuford's, his daddy. You remember those days back when you were teaching at Burleigh and how horrified you were when you saw blood in the creek and I told you where it came from. You remember? Beuford had a direct sewer line to the creek when he was embalming someone.

Yes, I was at Teddy's wake, but I just stayed for a few...

My lord what a crowd. He was only fifty-six. Wild as a billy goat. And all those Kellogs crying and shuffling around. Lewis glued a mustache on Teddy to give him some hair after all that chemo. Seems like all I do now is go to funerals and weddings and bowl on Tuesday nights with the girls. You know I'm seventy-five now. And Paul is hardly able to walk any more. Arthritis in his legs. I think he has it in his brains, too. I have to tell him what day it is over and over. Ever since the John Birch Chapter disbanded in Bardstown he's lost interest in things. You better be glad he can't get out enough to see the back of your car. I heard them over at the funeral home talking about your bumper stickers. I just don't see how anyone can say anything bad about President Bush. Iraq flying those planes into those big buildings like that. They can just use their opinions as enemas, I tell you. Oh, did you hear about what they're going to do if Hillary is elected? Make Mexico another state! Then we'll all have to learn Spanish. Just take over...

Evelyn. Let's talk about something else. Have you been reading anything interesting? I've just finished *The Black Book* by Orham Pamuk who won the Nobel Pri...

Those books that win those prizes are just trash. I wouldn't waste my time with any of them. I tried a few of those books that Oprah recommends, but Paul won't let me bring one in the house. You know how he is. We had to stop getting the Courier because it is so communist. He calls it *The Communist Journal.*

Evelyn, do you have a computer?

Oh, my god! I hope you don't have one of those things. All that nasty...

What do you think I used to write my book? A typewriter? Legal pads?

Well, I just thought you maybe had someone else type it up...

Evelyn, have you heard any good jokes? You remember how you used to embarrass me half to death with your jokes when I was first teaching at...

Oh, I've got to go. Paul is hollering that someone is driving up in the driveway.

Click.

Hunched-Up Woman

This bit of verse - is it poetry? - is about a street woman I observed while waiting to see an injured friend in the ER of University Hospital. Needing attention, she went from being an old woman to a whining child.

What is it like
to be a street person
grown old
and now needy
as a child

Hunched-Up Woman

Having suffered
all the prizes of betrayal in life
she made a well practiced entrance
past security
to triage
and
toothless
demanded her right
to be seen
to be touched by healing hands

"I'm sick!" she proclaimed
her chin up and out
her tits would be too
but they were asleep on her chest

Speaking into the microphone box
"I vomit!" the withered crone announced
gray strings for hair
sags for a face
and glittery glassy eyes
summarizing her self

"I bomick!"
now like the whine of a child
needing to climb onto a lap

The door buzzed open
for our little hunched-up woman
at the big city hospital

Sons and Fathers

My best work I think - an old man understanding fatherhood at long last. Earlier versions of this story first appeared in *LEO*, the winner of the Short Fiction contest, Jan. 28, 2008. I also included it in my novel, *Emerson Avery, That Latin Teacher*, 2009. It is mostly fiction, linear prose with a single point of view. There are some surreal elements.

Sons and Fathers

We are standing in the road, the two brothers and I. Not a smooth road for real traffic. Just a rough, curving, dead-end lane once an ancient toll pike of hand-cracked stones and now by-passed by the highway farther up beyond the tree line. Below us, the old trail, retaining the rutted impressions of wagon wheels, curls down the hill into secondary growth. I hear the bells from the nearby monastery calling for prayer. It is more distant but on the same road where the Donkey Tree is. "Everbody here'bouts knows the Donkey Tree," the taller brother tells me.

The sun is dropping below the ridge, but there remains sufficient light - our eyes and mouths clear to us. We stand at least an arm's length from each other. Perhaps *pose* is a better word than *stand*. Posing, slaunchwise as men do among relaxed male company. The trinity of us. I, the old man, favoring my right leg, with my shoulders back and hands in back pockets. The two men, the brothers, watching me, their bodies supple and rough hewn. Their voices sounding blood kin to their t-shirts and boots and blue jeans. Showing polite deference to me. "Mister Avery," they call me. Judging by their crust-edged hands and faces, both are in their thirties. The younger one, Gan, has lived a harsher life than Dice, I think. Each one chained to his separate indenture.

Mysteriously, under my eyes, they seem to enlarge and contract alternately. And, looking at them, I imagine the two as small boys playing "Hurt and Kiss." One squeezing a finger of the other until that one cries tears. "You gotta make real tears," they insist. Then the squeezer kisses the finger to absolve the pain. Back and forth as I had done long ago with my brother. A game of other as self.

I am here. We are here. In the rurals. An incestuous seeming place relying on all things familiar. And many in this population retain the tongueless mind-sets of their elders - the hugeness and danger of fathers, their necessity to be harsh.

For these brothers, I realize their final choice in living was the status quo. Sharing immobility and acceptance that they have come as far as they could. Drop out at sixteen and drift around from one fuck-up to another. Marriages. Jobs. Hopes that have been abandoned and forgotten. Ignorance. An occasional bright moment. Never enough money. Not hearing the music of Time sliding past. Life is desperate. Don't think about it. Don't think. And never get in a hurry.

Some years back, I was a teacher of their father, now dead. He was a boy then. Before he spent time in prison. And now his sons - although fully grown men, I think of them as boys - stand with me. Both slender in muscular ways. Dice smoking a cigarette. Gan gnawing at a troublesome fingernail now and again. Hardened men. The kind who are content to know little of other places. Both of them bearing the rugged countenance of drugs and booze. Of disruption and solitude. Of perpetual anxiety - which softens while we visit.

Off in the cedars are lights from Gan's trailer, one end sagging to the ground. He tells me his daughter moved out recently to be with her boyfriend. And Dice teases with adagio tempo, "An' yew know whut! Last year his old lady divorced him. I seen her drivin' off waving her middle finger out the winder." At that, the boys grin at each other, sharing their amusement at its recall.

They are close. "We visit of an evening about this same time." Come together and say little, I think. Share some weed and drink a beer or two. An assurance. Like the monastery bells. A place to be at the end of the day.

I drove here from the city to buy some pot from Gan. Home-grown is better. That delicious incense able to repel the hurts. The aroma of green hay with a touch of skunk. And I paid him for the quarter bag with Dice standing off to the side, attentive while avoiding the appearance of watching.

Our transaction was in Gan's dirt driveway hidden from the road by scrub cedars. Then we moved casually out to the scrumbly blacktop for a few moments of respectful conversation in the open space there. I am trusted even though I no longer belong here, in the rurals. But they credit me for having been a teacher of their father and once hunted coons with him and his older uncles on a night of low clouds and light, sharp sleet. The time the dogs treed an albino coon out on a limb of the Donkey Tree, its shape a fierce looking metamorphosis, a local object of high superstitions. Even today, that night hunt and kill are talked about by local hunters, imbedded in their set of lore.

Over there, to the side of their grandmother's house - the altar of that family - Dice's little boy is wrestling with the yellow dog. On her lawn. Both one-third grown. Tumbling. Scruffling. Yipping. Popping up and rolling over one another. Chasing. Running in circles. At times, instead of a flaxen haired boy and yellow dog, I see two young boys. Or is it two puppies? Free. Each of the same mind.

I comment to the brothers, "Look at them. That must be the highest form of happiness." The brothers look at the boy and the dog. I watch their eyes, Dice and Gan's, working over my words. Attaching them to the boy and the dog. A slight lifting nod of agreement from both.

The security light at the driveway to the grandmother's house comes on. First a hum. Then a yellow uncertainty before turning moon white. Each brother shifts his stance. A scruffling of boots. A one-step. A two-step. I hear the bark of their heels. Not restlessness. Just prevention of stagnation. Though they are a little apart from me, now and then they tilt closer. Then away. I catch how they glance at each other. There is a wordless, lifelong intimacy that bonds the two.

As we look, the boy, oblivious of us, stands with his arms out. And he twirls. A spinning top. The pup sits back and studies this. Puzzled. Its head cocked. The boy lifts his arms toward the security light. We hear the tolling from the monastery again. Then he begins hurling his arms for greater inertia to twirl and, in moments, tumbles to the grass. His eyes agoggle and unmindful of the dog.

We are remembering our own times, I think. Images of trust and freedom and silly fun wavering in the backs of our minds. Then the pup rocks back - and pounces on the boy. Their open joy resuming.

To them, to the brothers, I am a curiosity from the lands beyond their lives. But having taught their father and people up and down the roads and lanes of this area, I have their tacit passport for safe entry and trust.

In this setting at low dusk, my awareness of this child - and his father and uncle beside me - rings stronger and more vivid. The idea of paternity surfaces - the continuance of seed, that endless and easy flow of generations. In my head I catch a scene of a father walking in tall grass. His young boys trying to stay close. Leaping up again and again. Their heads bobbing above the grass to keep him in sight.

Now, in my last years, I understand. It was here in the rurals where I encountered that sharp-edged reality: a son's youth is his father's envy - a son's growth is his father's decline - a son's friends are his father's rivals. And I recall the father of Dice and Gan.

I earlier inspected them for traces of their father as I remembered him in school back in the unruly 1960's. A teasing sort of kid in bib overalls and boots sometimes redolent of a dairy barn. At other times, the faint odor of wet wood ashes about him. Hands of a laboring man. A smooth face trying to look older - his life already sculpted there. A sturdy boy with smoke blue eyes and harsh eyebrows - like his sons, Gan and Dice. A ninth grader not quite sixteen biding his time to be an adult man.

He was fascinated by our Opportunity Class and was usually the first to rush in. At the beginning of the second week, just before the others came rumbling in, he showed me his new Barlow knife. To impress me. To relate to me. A gentle offer of trust. The sharing of his pride and a step into the shy courtship of a boy awed by an unthreatening older man.

In class he scrambled letters in words - *god* for *dog*.

It was the superintendent who anointed this English class *Opportunity Class*. My instructions from on high were, "Do whatever you can to encourage their language skills. Most of them will drop out as soon as they can. See if you can improve their reading, writing, and speaking."

I knew about being different. About belittlement and dismissal in the eyes of my own people. And vicious teasing and abuse for being dissimilar. About frustration and social predation. The cruelties of older males. Thus, the idea of this classroom captivated me. A potential means of atonement maybe. I would use whatever tricks I could to energize these kids. Set it up so that each one might find pride in individual ingenuity. Twenty-nine troubled boys. No girl among them. Hardly a one could read beyond basic service words. But they loved nature. And guns. Messing around with motors and electric circuits. Stories about dogs and horses and hot rods.

Two of them had killed their drunken fathers - to protect their mothers. Both in bleak mid-winter. One with his father's shotgun. The other with his mother's butcher knife. The grand jury did not indict either of them. However, their paternal grandmothers did, one even placing an announcement in the local paper each year, the anniversary of her son's death, "murder" she termed it memorializing his demise by the hand of her grandson. When time came for first one boy and then the other, with dark circles under eyes, to return to school, no one in our class treated them differently.

Each now walking with a different step. Both of them disarmed of their fathers.

The boys in that class amazed me in their practiced obdurance against academic learning. So I had them bring in snakes and turtles and fish and worms and frogs. Reindeer moss, too. For our terrarium. To nourish and observe. For dissecting. For learning words words words.

I went coon hunting with several of them and got to know their families and ways. Their values. Their superstitions. Every one of them firmly believed in ghosts. And God less firmly. Each boy had a dog. They all knew first hand about death. Yet, when I read *Old Yeller* to them, as one they sniffled and teared up quietly at the end. Along with me.

Standing in the hush of evening, I told Gan and Dice recollections of their dad, about the time I left Opportunity Class for a few minutes and came back to find all of the boys, including him, in a circle holding hands. I thought, "Now what?" Then I understood. They had been waiting for any chance to play with an Army surplus telephone generator I had on my desk. The kind that you might notice in a war movie - a soldier in a fox hole cranking the box to connect with headquarters for artillery support. I took in the spectacle of this class unselfconsciously holding hands. One boy held a finger on the anode and another boy pressed a thumb firmly to the cathode so the current would travel around the circle of boys. Another little fellow, the one terrified of electrical shocks, cranked up the generator sending out twelve volts around the circle. The smaller boys experienced the jolts. Yelling. But the bigger boys looked blank. That is, until Scaredy Cat revved up the generator to as fast as he could go, his tongue to one side of his lips and his eyes sparks of happiness. That's when the big ones also leaped and lurched and squalled out. All of them as one feeling the needle-like electrical impulses.

Another great moment of learning had slipped in on

them. About electrical resistance. And I bragged loudly to them about how they cooperated with each other. That different kind of power.

These reminiscences of an old man feeling compassion for the past - and passing on special memories.

When Christmas break came, I asked who would take the cage and pair of love birds home since I would be out of town. The father of Gan and Dice pleaded and begged louder than the others. So I appointed him. Drove him to his home after school. Way out in the country. Not far from the monastery and the Donkey Tree. Proud as a tom turkey he marched, maybe "paraded" is the better word, into his mother's house - talking and cooing to the birds and looking back at me over his shoulder.

And when school resumed in January, in he shuffled with the cage. Empty. He looked at my feet and began lightly crying, holding back sobs. I held his shoulders at arm's length, looking down at him, and asked what had happened. Between gulps and sniffling, he said, "Saturty last, I let them birds out to fly around in the house and my cat ate 'em up." Solemn looks from the other boys. We had lost members of our family - and strengthened an understanding of food-chains and natural selection.

There in the country road, I told those stories to Dice and Gan. But I left out that their father had cried. The three of us cloaked under the free and happy sounds of the boy and yellow dog on their grandmother's lawn. The boy taking a moment to lie stretched flat on his back in the grass. Arms out to his sides. The dog wondering about this. Waiting for more.

Gan's eyes went to his boots, inspecting them before lifting his head to his brother. Grinning. The air between them busy. "Old Dad, he sure didn't need no embalmin' fluid when he died, did he?"

Each of us there a son, never coddled by a father.

Lobo

Poetic writing about rugged individualism and independence,
values that I, an introvert, admire most highly.

The lyrics of an introvert
do not resemble
the grunts and squawks
from an extrovert

Shy hunters
have other needs

Lobo

Even a lone wolf
once belonged to a pack

During dreams
protests of memory
I recall my people
and that simple and strangling life
of home
and neighbors

Privacy did not exist
and it was that
the discovery of solitude
which sent me
on my journey
gloriously free
to discover my self

A shy hunter
in blind struggle against rescue
always chooses life
alone

Even a lone wolf
belonged to a pack
once

Dead Child with Open Eyes

This short story, which employs magic realism, is pure linear fiction with a single point of view. It is eerie and painful, the interior workings of a frightened man in deep grief.

After a death
reality becomes distorted
and truth is questionable

Dead Child with Open Eyes

I was shaving and intent upon the process, watching the safety razor swipe away the white layer of foam, feeling the little tugs of the blade as it mowed through my whiskers. The mirror was becoming slightly steamed, so I toweled away the moisture. Looking into it, I saw her, the reflection of a little girl standing beside me. I was more than jolted by this. I leaped and turned to her, yelling. But she was gone.

Five years before that my wife and I were living in another state. Enjoying the first months of our life together, and I, at last, able to find redress from my miserable childhood. On a quiet Saturday night I heard her gasp and felt her body jerk beside me. Two men were in our bedroom. One jabbed the point of a large knife to my jugular, and the other picked her up and threw her to the floor, leaping on her. In moments we were both restrained by duct tape. Yards of it. After being forced to watch them strip and rape her, one of them slit her throat while the other man held me close to her and pulled back my eyelids so I had to witness her death. Her eyes were staring into mine. The killers were laughing. Giggling. Their sweaty, unwashed stench overpowering. Will I ever not hear the zipping sound of the blade opening her neck?

Now, five years later, after years of therapy, I am accepting of that night and the loss and death of her. With the help of a good shrink and an effective drug, I am independent again. My affect is said to be "normal." And I agree - I have attained equanimity at last. However, since that sickening night, there have been several eerie occurrences - unreal sightings. Each of them, I decided, was the product of seeing her death, her body sagging onto the pool of blood. Her eyes watching me. Each fraction of a second an incipient mutilation of my mind.

The first hallucinal sighting occurred some days after her murder. This first one involved a bus. I was back in the city. Standing at a corner waiting for the light to change. A metro bus hissed and grumbled slowly past, its passengers sitting like mannequins looking at nothing in particular. And there, seated toward the middle of the bus, was my wife. Eyes half open, she turned her head with the sure movement of a puppet. To look at me. To fix me with the same relaxed expression her face bore on the coroner's slab. Her low lidded brown eyes now piercing and preternaturally blue instead. The interior of my mind crumbled and avalanched. The yelling I heard was my own. People were looking at me as I was screaming and flapping my arms above my head. *Another man gone crazy on a city sidewalk!* I fled to my car glommed over with terror and cold sweat.

Do the inhabitations of grief and fear ever end? And guilt also? Why was I the one to survive?

Can you blame me? In the weeks following, I jumped into a geographic cure - I packed and moved to a quiet rural county in Kentucky. To an apartment. But it would take several years of painful work with the shrink and finding the best drug before I could buy a house of my own and return to the classroom.

Some months after beginning therapy, deep into night as I was lying in bed looking up at the ceiling during that pleat of consciousness before slipping into sleep, while studying the colorless swipe of lesser gray from the tiny hall light, a collection of generic faces appeared above me. They were transparent in tones of gray. Glassine faces of people unknown to me. Epicene countenances that swirled together in a roiling stew of bubbling up and of receding into the background. Ready for mental play with any delusions that might come along, I watched them with amusement.

With my mind's eye grabbing one face, I made it smile and then laugh in equal amusement to my own. Next, using mental force, I made its features mutate into that of a young girl's. A sweet child playing by herself. I was able to control this parade of phantom guests that had come to accompany me into sleep. I thought of *The Christmas Carol* by Dickens and that bit about the rotten pea in Scrooge's soup. And I remembered a term from psychology: *hypnogogia*. I was, indeed, having a *hypnogogic* reaction. My brain chemistry along with the drug I had been prescribed were playing an eerie game with me. Taunting me.

Realizing this and satisfied that I was not insane again, I rolled to my side. After a few moments, the faces evaporated under the forces of reality, and, again secure in the safety and comfort of my new home, I went to sleep.

For four years, I was employed in a library. A small town public library. This was a critical time for me - the period of adjustment while I worked with the shrink and my body settled on the correct dose of an antidepressant. With her permission, my shrink's, I bought a small house near the school where I had been hired to teach.

When did I see the dead girl in the mirror? It was sometime in February. A cold snap had left ten inches of snow and ice, and we had no school for a week in that rural area. The air crisp and clean. I had gotten up late, eaten a bit, did the crossword puzzle, and finished washing the dishes while listening to *All Things Considered*. My little house felt chilly to me. In the bathroom, with the door closed, I took inventory of my naked body in the full length mirror on the door. A quick examination of my body confirmed that I was standard issue and all the parts were present, but what about my interior. My most vulnerable part. My psyche. Looking into my eyes, I recognized the potentials of my dis-ease. A man toiling, still, with guilt and fear. And this spell of being house-bound was weakening my defenses. With verve, standing there, I set a firm goal to decode those negative potentials by washing away the torpor of cabin fever's onset and the grief that had become a part of me. Nothing like a good hot shower to nurture contact with reality and regain stable mental health.

After a languorous shower and a rough toweling, I assumed the shaving position at the sink, leaning forward toward the mirror with my upper thighs against the edge of the sink. The lather was in place, and I had made the first smooth and comforting swipe from right ear to jaw. It was at that moment that I noticed her, the little girl beside me. She was solemn, like a dead child with open eyes and with long, limp brunette hair. Her eyes were dark, lifeless, and she was wearing a red dress with a modest white collar. I leaped and screamed, and she was gone.

Where did this hallucination come from? This bit of unreality? And why in my home?

School resumed two days later after the roads were finally cleared. We were studying Poe's *The Raven* that day, and I read it to the class with all the drama I could manage, barely whispering in some spots and screaming in agony in others. "Chewing the scenery," as they say. My young folks were electrified and wide-eyed.

One of the neighborhood boys was in that eighth grade reading class. It was after class that Kevin, the neighbor, came up and told me, quietly, almost in the voice of a confession, that a little girl had died in my house the year before. He said a family had lived there. She had been sick was all he knew. Her parents moved away a few weeks after she died. Then I moved in.

To say that I felt surges of intense tingling up and down my spine would be an understatement. When I returned to my little home that afternoon, I could barely force myself to enter. Like being near a large sleeping animal. Was I no longer safe there, or had the migrations of my mind transformed it into a private chamber of horrors? Was it a place anointed by some grisly history?

I could not, I would not allow that affect to be a part of my living or a part of my home. I would bar any residual raven of death from occupying my dwelling or my mind - to allow belief to take the place of knowledge.

Once inside, bristling with the tingles of possibly being watched by some unknown force, I rushed about turning on all the lights and fully opening each curtain to the unforgiving brilliance of sunlight off the snow. With a slight tremor in my hand, I put on the record of Bartok's *Concerto for Orchestra* - vibrant, strong, and real, pulling reality back into my place with this music - the same place I knew where a little girl had died. An innocent girl who was, somehow, becoming coupled with the images of my blameless wife. The debris of our married life pelting me again like hail announcing a tornado. Moving through the rooms of my house, I knew I would have to work assiduously to be reinstated into the arms of sanity - even though reality has a way of being badly organized.

Looking for any sign of the previous owners, I inspected each room, and my search revealed nothing out of the ordinary. Wall by wall there was no anomaly, no secret place, no magic button for a hidden doorway to the other side. No fetid odors seeping up from the floor or down from the attic.

Finally, there, in my bedroom closet, I found it. About five feet up from the floor - an unevenness in the drywall. It had the shape of a rectangle about twelve inches high by eight inches wide, large enough for a face. To my eye, it appeared that a section of the drywall had been cut out and later replaced leaving some unevenness where the seams were not sanded down smoothly. Electrified with the frisson of discovery of an eerie secret, I immediately went into the guest room on the other side of my closet. Nothing unusual there. The wallpaper had a red and black paisley pattern to it.

There was no unevenness to my touch or to my eye, even at the area where the cut had been made in my closet.

My curiosity leaped to high alert. Was something hidden? A secret portal for some perversion between the parents' room and the smaller bedroom? Could it have been a little girl's bedroom? The same child with the dead eyes looking at me in the bathroom? I realized there are chambers in ordinary lives, in commonplace places, and in humdrum times that are never entered - let alone mentioned. Were the chambers of this house speaking to me through the mystery of this girl? And were they blood flavored? I was now fully obsessed by a single focus: to replace fantasy with reality, to open the sealed door to whatever haunted this house, and to exorcise it. And, especially, to slice it from my mind. What had happened here? Why did the apparition of a dead child appear to me in my small bathroom with the door closed? Was she trying to tell me something? Did the house retain echoes of some unsettled macabre secret which soundly defeated the Sears catalogue pictures of the happy family, everyone standing or sitting around smiling and beautiful?

Within the hour, I had removed the patched place in my closet - the rectangular piece of drywall there. Now I was looking at the backside of my guest room's drywall. A dime-sized spot caught my eye, a place that had been resealed with putty. With painstaking care I scraped out the putty. It narrowed to a tiny point at its exit, and a minuscule ray of light leaked to me from the guest room on the other side.

After a search, I found a common pin and inserted it into that hole. I entered the guest room. There on the wall, exactly where I knew it would be, was the silver shaft of the pin sticking through the middle of a black area of the wall paper pattern. Without the pin, the tiny hole would not be noticeable. I touched the tip of the pin and flicked it as if I were flicking the vision of a voyeur's eyeball leering from the other side. Fortified by this intelligence, this refutation of any supernatural fantasy or hallucination of a dead girl, I returned to my bedroom closet with its secret peephole. Obviously, there had been something amiss in that family, the former owners. And, somehow, I had been drawn into it.

Staring at the pinhole, I decided there would be no more disavowal of howling reality by the playful comforts of fantasy, of the convenient belief that there are spirits and afterlives. Armed with this, I could feel my fear beginning to vaporize - those horrors that had forced me to stagger again up to the edges of insanity. It was apparent that an adult had been peeking at whoever slept in the guest room. Possibly, even worse, maybe a sexual pervert had taken up leering at the young girl in the privacy of her own room and space. None of this, however, explained my hallucination in the bathroom even though it placed it in the light of reality. Could the explanation possibly be echoes of an event in this house that, with my accelerated subjectivity, triggered my mind to see a dead child with open eyes?

I was ready to make the repairs in the closet and, in my mind's thinking, chortle with amusement - to move on with my new, more stable life. Write. Treat myself to a hard workout every day and be ready for deep sleep at night.

I went into the shed, found a piece of drywall, cut it, and shaped it to fit the panel I had destroyed. With materials in hand for this operation, I remembered the pin. Using needle-nosed pliers, I extracted it, not unmindful of the image of someone's eye being there. A slender pin. A ray of light. An innocent child possibly being ogled through this hole. I leaned over, inserted my face into the space, and looked through the tiny opening - through the yellow dot of light and into the next room.

On the bed knelt a man - a naked man hovering over a small girl. Her mouth taped shut.

Ethan Talbot Carney

Imagine the town bum around 1880 in a rural Kentucky hamlet, a forty-ish perpetually inebriated loafer leaning back against a board fence and watching what little activity there is. He is talking to himself - thinking out loud - his voice somewhat congested and with a permanent whine to it.

It amounts to an historical bit of fiction that I spent many hours researching.

Ethan Talbot Carney
A Monologue

Setting: Circa 1880 in a rural Kentucky town.
Speaker: Forty-ish, inebriated town loafer leaning his back against a board fence watching what little activity there is in town. He is talking to himself - thinking out loud - his voice somewhat congested and with a whistle sometimes before he hawks up some spit.

Looka him over yonder walkin' toward the bank. He never be swole gutted. We the same age I think. Him and me. Ole Ethan. Mr. Ethan Talbot Carney. I 'member he done told on me when I hid behind the outhouse to smoke during playtime up at the schoolhouse on the hill. Mean old bat Mizzrus Plump made me go get a stick to whup me with and sent me back two more times 'fore I brung one thick enuff to suit her. I'll tell more about that goodie two-shoes Ethan later. No whuppin' stop me from smoking' though. Still rolling 'em when I get my hands on any loose tobaccer. If I don't got no store-bought, I make a visit to some 'baccer barn and get me some dried leaves. That suff'd tear the hide off your lungs. But whiskey ain't no good without somepin' ta smoke. An' that white dog Gran-pa makes needs tobaccer to dull the burn and give it taste.

Pretty damn quiet-like. I jest sittin' yhere my back to a board fence outside the pool hall watchin' this little town go by. Not even a dog fight. Warm sunshine day. Upstanding town folks ignorin' me as usual. They 'member them days back in the war when I was somebody. They 'member the Home Guard. Scared of us.

Ethen, he talking to the preacher's wife. He's that very goody-two-shoes got my ass whupped in school. Look it him there, walking up to the bank like he ain't got no care in the world. Tipping his hat to her. Be damned if he didn't bow to her, too. Gentleman, he is. Oh, yeah. Makin' eyes and showin' manners to a preacher's wife. Pretty little thing. But a person can't fart in this little burg without it being passed on. I bet word on the way right now that she stopped and talked to Ethan.

I knowd all them Carneys. Most of 'em fine folks. I believe it was his uncle Rudolph, that ole blatherskite, born a sonabitch and died a sonabitch, got cut up under the Louisville Pike bridge playing craps with them boys from over round Tarpit and St. Jude. You'd a thought ole Rudy was the President the ways them Carneys carried on at his burial. My buddies and me had to drop our eyes when old Mizzrus Carney jump up on his casket and starts a-prayin' an' a-singin' an' moanin'. But afterwards they had a fine, fine dinner on the grounds at the church. Nary a soul there from St. Jude nor Tarpit. I think everbody from around here was there but Bob the Blacksmith, and he woulda came if he hadden-na got the back-door screamin' trots so bad that day. Buggies and wagons and horses and mules all over. I kep my eye on that one Carney girl, Marybelle. That one with the burnin' red hair. She give me a plate of chicken, an' it were her very own plate. Pretty good tending-to for a sot like me. Scared me I might be in love so bad I didn't even 'member them next three days. Jest floatin' around humming.

Look a' him. Still looks like a young man. Stands tall. Keeps his chin up. Happy eyes. Strong body. Dresses well. Got that fine, I mean really fine looking wife, Nelda. Oh, yeah, Miz Nelda. Can't imagine them two at it. Ethan and Nelda. I bet I got something that'd make her real happy. He too fine a gentleman. Hair just so. I look like a bum next to him. Well, I guess I am, sorta.

Now I ponder it, though, I got a strong recollection about him. Ever since the war when I was part of the Home Guard, I just don't give a shit about life. When Mr. Davis's conscription came, Ethan was a young gentleman farmer out with his pa, and Papa bought him a man to take his place soldiering. Ebo it was. Them Carneys didn't have no trouble with us Town Guard or Mr. Davis's men or even when the Yanks was in control around here. Their colonel stayed out at the Carney homestead, and they treated him like royalty. Been a few years since then. Maybe fifteen, twenty years, I reckon. War ended and the Home Guard ended, too.

That been the last time I got me some fine young tail. Out Cooney Neck Fork at a place where them burned-out Bradleys was a-squattin'. We rode in an' capturred their cow and three pigs an' all his whiskey an' his wagon. Tied them squatters up and tooken their girl and had us a fine time down on Liberty Creek. Her just asquealin'. Yes, sir-ee. A fine ol' time!

You know, some people just look good from any direction. I ain't interested in Ethan the way a man might admire a woman, but he's sure a fine looking man even if I say so. Some people got it easy from the time they pullin' on they mamma's tit. His pa with all that land and a fine farm and he's richer than Queen Victoria. Ethan ain't got no brothers to split it up with, an' he got all them sisters to help run the place. Most of their slaves stayed on after the war, and they live better than me. Sure do. Ethan, he stayed on the big farm and Ebo soldiered for him. Ethan got schooled like his pa. Smart. Got real manners. I ain't never heard no one say nothing bad about him nor his pa. They say that Ethan might run for judge next term.

I shore know something nobody else arounst-about chere knows. 'Ceptin' Ebo. He done made it back from the war, and he and his Ginger lived in one of the cabins. Ebo, he raised up there and were Ethan's whippin' boy. An' everbody knowd he Ethan's half-brother. From Papa Carney.

Back jus' after the war I spied on the Carney place for a fortnight. Hid in the fields, under their outbuildings, an'even in their cellar one night. I wanted to know they secrets. Had my eye on one of Ethan's young sisters, too. Marybelle. The one with red hair. Heard tell copperheads so hot they'll burn the hide off your pecker.

One night I was in the corn field up close to the big house where the family liven. They bedrooms was up on the second and third floors. The Carney slaves livin' in their row of cabins b'hind the big house. Usually I never seed much goin's-on after good-an' dark, but that one night I spied a man come out the back of the house and go to the grape arbor. Mizzrus Carney had that arbor built special, an' it had two big arches and a swing an' some benches. She had the grape vines dug up and let ivy grow around the swing. Shady and nice, especially in the summer. She'd sit there and enjoy the shade on hot days. Watchin' birds and keepin' cool in the breeze.

Well, I seen that man go into the arbor, and then another man come down from the cabins. He also go into the arbor. I waited to go see what they was up to. No movement and no noises. So I tooken my time and snuckt over to wheres I could be hidden an' still could see them in there. They was a little bit of moonlight, but mostly I could kindly make out the outlines of them against the sides of the big house. I 'member hearing the old owl hootin' back over by the barns. An' whippoorwills calling back and forth. An' it not like I ain't seen something like this 'fore, but I was sure enough surprised to see them two buck naked. It was Ethan and his old whippin' boy, Ebo. Them two growed up together. Ebo light skinned. An' Ethan pale as a ghost in the dark. Them two in the arbor behaving like two young boys b'hind the barn on a Sunday afternoon. Thay-Law! What would people say 'bout that, and him maybe runnin' for jedge?

I was grinning' an' watchin' an seen a dark shadow move along by the edge of the corn. A woman. I hunkered down more and waited. It were Ginger. Feisty Gingersnap. She were canny as a mink an' spying on her man, Ebo. I held in my breath a-wonderin' what she gonna do. She took still as a stump, then she lit into the arbor, an' I seen the flash of a knife in her hand. She musta gone take 'em both on. Strange. She wattn't screaming 'r squalling in her attack. I heard 'em tussling' an' gruntin', an' then it got quieter than night. My heart pumpin'. Here I was spyin' an' half skeert to take in a breaf a' air. Two standin' and one on the ground. Two men astandin'. I watcthin' 'em awonderin'. Ebo in Ethan's arms shakin' and sobbin'. Ethan pattin' and aswayin' with him. They do this awhile, then put they clothes back on. Ebo go off and come back with a shovel. They talk a little real quiet-like, and then they pick up Gingersnap's corpse and go off toward the big trees. I seen enough.

After a bit, I go on back to my room in town. All these years I never tell nobody noways. My big secret. Soon word out Gingersnap done run off in the night to some a her kin down in Georgia. Ebo no choice, but only stay here where he growed up, people say. He stay close to Ethan, I say.

No sir, I never tell nobody 'bout that night. Figure some day I might use that bit of news to git me a little ol' crack at Marybelle Carney. If Ethan, he run for judge, maybe he make Marybelle give me some jist to keep me quiet, don't ya' know.

But I don't know about that Ebo.

End of monologue.

A Folk Tale in Threes

With a bow to the ancient myths of Greece and Rome, this is fiction, perhaps qualifying as a short story. The mystical numbers have always intrigued me: three, four, nine, and twelve. Three in this case - the family: father, mother, and child, and our confounding ideas of destiny, fate and fortune that remain alive and well for most people even in this age of science and information.

The mystical number three
and its possibilities
for explaining ordinary lives

Is there any truth
to destiny
fate
and fortune
Charlie Brown

A Folk Tale in Threes

Once upon a time in a place nearby, very nearby, there were three geese. The only geese for many miles in any direction. Their home was the small spring-fed lake near the ruins of the old distillery. They were identically feathered birds with necks like ballet dancers and feet like Army recruits. No one in Fairfield or for miles around bothered to give them names because each one was indistinguishable from the other two, and they moved with one accord and one purpose in all matters. Somewhat like a gaggle of twelve year old unsupervised girls set loose in a large mall. The geese roamed around the town at will, and the local folks of Fairfield were careful of the geese. Always protecting them when necessary. For good luck.

"Don't run over the geese, Honey," Mom warned Wilbur, her seventeen year old son who slowed down and gave plenty of room for the community's geese to waddle across the dirt road in front of the truck. And he wondered about a scene that flashed in his mind. *Just what would it look like if I hit all three at once on a cool, clear day with nobody watching? I bet white feathers would fly up into the air like a burst pillow. Yeah!*, he thought with a narrow-eyed look of malice.

So, let's get to the story part. As I said of the local people, the three geese also didn't bother with names for each other. Of course not. They could only honk and hiss. It was the destiny of these birds to be the same both in name, or lack of it, and in life. Did you notice that word, *destiny*? Jumped right out at you, didn't it? A troublesome idea to me. How about you? It has its hooks in the ancient world and its many mythologies, *n'est-ce pas?*

Interesting, though, there were also three elderly sisters who lived down the road in the Old Parker Place which had been their father's and grandfather's and great-grandfather's. No longer an active farm, the old house was in need of paint and repairs. Unlike the geese, however, these three sisters had names. Names which mimicked those superstitious words for the gullible: *destiny, fate, and fortune.* An eternal complicity, the three of them.

One of them, who resembled a harpy, loved to spin wool into thread - sometimes with tangles and knots. Her name was Clotho - Clothy for short. She was ever on the lookout, as each of her sisters was, for different fibers to spin into thread. Some of it became thick yarn and others became thread of different gauges, even as thin as silk. Her sisters admired the skills Clothy had developed as a spinner. However, the three of them had a quiet, running disagreement over how she never washed a single dish in the house. Never. "Clothy, you are just mean and ornery!" the other two nagged.

The second sister, a harridan, stringy haired and bossy, took it upon herself to keep track of the newly spun thread - bobbins of it. Each one with a different, exact measurement of the thread's length. Her name was Lachesis, Lakey for short. She would take the new thread and hold it in the morning sunlight for a careful examination to determine its special quality. When she was satisfied, Lakey directed the third sister to the exact spot to snip it so it could be twined onto individual spools. Neither of the other sisters dared to challenge her skill at measuring the length of any thread - long, short, thick, thin, raw, or dyed. By the way, Lakey went by the name Titty at home.

The third sister, the embodiment of a crone, after she had cut the thread's carefully measured length and had wound it again, placed each spool on a special shelf in the parlor. When people came to the kitchen door in the late evening, knocked timidly and stated their needs for a particular type of thread, she made them stand there at the door in the shadows while she strode importantly to the parlor and came back with a specific thread. Oddly, though, what she presented to the customer might not be at all what was asked for. But as soon as she presented it, the buyer looked it over and went on and on about how it was exactly what was needed. Maybe they were affected by this sister's eyes. Or it could be that the thread itself held some unseen quality which had a curious effect on them. This sister had one white eye and one that beamed black light into the faces of those who visited. Her name was Atropos. Troper for short. Her hands were gnarled and had a spattering of green warts on the tops of her fingers. "Troper, why don't you cut back your fingernails and scrape out the dirt under them?" the other sisters often inquired. This forever made Troper smile with a private satisfaction, blink her good eye, and scratch at a wart on her thumb.

There you have it: Clothy, Lakey, and Troper - the strange women down the road at the Old Parker Place. Renowned to all thereabout in and around little Fairfield. The same distinction as the geese. Especially by the children and young folks who kept a careful lookout for the three geese and for the three old Parker women.

Now, let's see. Three geese without names. Three old ladies with two front names each.

But what's in a name anyway?

Interesting question.

Have you ever noticed that hearing a person's name brings up a long list of images and information: the named person's face, body shape, age, work, community involvement, house, deeds, family members and history, how they chew gum, and on and on. As if the name of a person somehow carries a record of that person's past destiny with it. And who they are today, not to mention who they will be for days and weeks and years. Odd, isn't it? Whenever a person in that area said the name of one the three sisters, a clear picture of her flooded the minds of the listeners. And along with the mental image were remembered smells and sounds and personal lore along with recollections of a strange tingling which raced around their necks and shoulders when they had visited the Old Parker Place. But when anyone mentioned the geese, it was a single goose that came to mind with no name attached to it. No waves of shivering. Only the shape and colors and goose sounds clear-cut in their minds.

So, try this on for size:

If a goose is in Fairfield, it has no name.
There are three geese in Fairfield.
Therefore, each has no name.

Or:

A person's name describes that person.
Each of the three old sisters has a name.
Therefore, each one is described by her name.

So what? you think to yourself. *Yeah, I recognize a simple syllogism when I see one. And these two are* modus ponens *syllogisms. What do the geese and the three old ladies have to do with this?*

Well, sit still and listen closely. Maybe having a name ensouls and empowers its owner. What if, someday, a fox gobbled up one of the geese or some hunter shot them and cooked them with apples and oranges and red wine for a feast. Life will go on the same. Those silly geese were pretty to look at and tasty to eat. But without names, they will be soon forgotten. They will remain the same in the minds of Fairfield's populace. They did not change the lives of anyone. But this can not be said of people, of humans, with names. People who had been children. Children who had been newborns. Newborns who had worn cloth containing thread from the three sisters at the Old Parker Place.

Clothy, Lakey, and Troper were certainly not three no-name geese. Their names entered the lives of almost every person thereabout. And their thread provided, somehow, the destiny of each child who wore their threads. Don't you see? What's in a name is one's destiny, fortune, lot, future, and fate. For generations, when people came to the kitchen door in the late evenings for lengths of thread, it was used to make articles of clothing, quilts, pillows, and handkerchiefs. Beautiful hand sewn items to finger and pat and shuff. Mostly for little newborns. Maybe to add a little rose or a button hole or a name to a collar. Even to weave into cloth. Booties. Crib blankets. Christening gowns.

Unknown to anyone, the thread of the old sisters bypassed DNA and time and place. It, instead, gave the wearer his or her future life, its length, and its smoothness and difficulties. In other words, the thread locked in the destiny, fate, and fortune of the newborn. There are those words again. Personally, I don't give any credence to such constructs. Not in this age of science and raging atrophy of theology and philosophy and ancient mythology.

What do you think about that, Charlie Brown?

Hum?

Does of it really matter?

Big Muncey

Over the years as a teacher, I have observed the rise and fall of school heroes and beauty queens. Usually one of each in every class. So, this short story is about one young man, Muncey, who has it all, it seems. It is entirely linear fiction from the narrator's point of view.

It must be difficult
to be a hero
a star
a role model
and then fall
into disgrace
in the eyes
and lives
of worshipful toadies
and adoring self

Big Muncey

They called him Big Muncey, his friends did around those rural parts in the late 1940's south of Louisville. Back in the time of small high schools in just about every town. Certainly, the name Edmond Campbell would have been too much of a mouthful, so the sound of it morphed like those entrenched family names that just don't suit the owners. His first name became softened to Edmunce and then, by the time he started growing like a weed in junior high, his classmates simply called him Muncey. Later in Chadwick High School he filled out and became six feet six inches of muscle and brawn and blarney. The basketball coach, who was also the history and drivers' training teacher, delighted in having a big bruiser on the team. And he began calling him Big Muncey. That name stuck with everyone except his parents and the older people who continued calling him Edmond, as was their way.

Don't be misled by any stereotypes of our modern day athletes. He did good work in school in spite of little interest in academics. His parents saw to that. But they contemplated no thoughts of college for their big son. One time during a basketball game, Big Muncey's father commented to the school principal as they watched a game standing together at the big door to the little gym, "He don't need no extra learning in no college." The principal agreed.

During his four years at Chadwick High School, Big Muncey enjoyed being the star basketball player and making "pretty good" grades. Also he set the school basketball record for points scored, including free-throws, and they remained unbroken even after the high schools became consolidated into one massive school at the county seat.

During his senior year, his hometown reeled in

excitement: their little school's team had won the regional semi-finals and now were set to play in the regional finals, a level of competition which that school had never come close to attaining. Word throughout town and all over the area that their very own little bitty Chadwick High School's team had an excellent chance of competing in the Kentucky State Basketball Tournament kept tongues wagging. For an unheard of, backwoods school team to go to State was considered slightly lower than guaranteed entrance to Heaven. Everywhere people, choked with disbelief, sputtered, "Just one more! They just gotta win one more. That big ole Campbell boy gonna take 'em all the way!"

Sadly, though, Big Muncey came down with mumps the day before the regional championship game. The team, without its leader, limped onto the floor at the big Elizabethtown gym and limped off in shame after a terrible trouncing.

You may ask: Whatever happens to last year's athletic stars and beauty queens in a tiny community? Does their fame live on? Maybe you remember that gorgeous Betty Bowers who won the Beauty Queen title for the Hog Growers' Association three years back? Now she has two sets of twins, stringy hair, a broken front tooth, and big ole titties hanging south. Former athletes don't fare much batter, if at all. Big Muncey's father, Mr. Campbell, not about to let his son turn into a pot-bellied fallen hero, an idler boring people with recollections of his stardom, announced to him the day after high school graduation, "Edmond, you're gonna work full time helping me with the milking and running the farm." The matter of a job, then, was settled, and it required hard, muscle-aching work, even for Big Muncey.

His lifelong buddies came by often. Now keep in mind, Chadwick was not a cosmopolitan crossroads. Most of the people living there came from families that had settled in that area as pioneers. Of Big Muncey's senior class of thirty-two, only two had moved in from elsewhere, and they were Army brats whose mothers were originally from Chadwick.

Edmond's friends often helped Big Muncey with chores on the farm. Mr. Campbell smiled to himself when he figured out how his son managed this. Big Muncey would say to one or the other of his pals, "Wonder if I could get you to give me a hand tomorrow for a li'l bit? I'll let you hep me with my milking (or whatever). Won't take long, then we can go..." Big Muncey would "let" so-and-so "hep." The old Tom Sawyer routine. If Muncey offered to "let" some of his buddies "hep" shovel ten years of horse manure out the horse stalls, his buddies would snatch the pitch fork and shovels from his hands and start digging. They needed his approval and friendship. He was Big Muncey, no ordinary person.

What is it about people so full of blarney? No one would deny that Big Muncey was a fine, strapping specimen of a young man. Not exactly handsome, but the way he walked and talked and commanded attention captivated his contemporaries, a following of younger folks, a handful of town drunks, and even the village idiot. Admiring girls giggled in his presence, and they ogled over his butt, high and strong, and his loose-legged walk. His voice sounded deep and resonant, and he effortlessly kept up a spiel of endless good humor to support his famous blarney. Rich dark brown hair covered his chest and arms, and this also seemed to give him more power and manliness than most guys. When he and his buddies were around a group of girls, if any unwelcomed lulls or awkward silences arose, they could rely on Big Muncey's wit, his sass and teases.

Muncey's banter lost no power even when just he and a few guys got together. And, in safe company, he could tell a dirty joke that left his buddies red faced and running in little circles haw-hawing - although they might have heard him tell it several times before. His thick eyebrows uplifted, Big Muncey the Marvelous would halt a conversation, thrust his head forward and, with sparkling eyes, ask, "Do you know what you get if you cross a midget and a prostitute?"

His idolaters would stop, process the images of a midget and a prostitute, and wait for the punch line thinking vague thoughts of sex, about sex that just might somehow be associated with Big Muncey.

"No. What?" some toady would always ask.

"Well, Dummy, you'd get a little fucker about this tall," indicating the height by holding one hand above the other with about twelve inches between. In the minds of the listeners, they related images of the "little fucker" to Big Muncey's rumored pride and joy, his male endowment. Then, obedient to the tempo of joke telling, they would laugh and fall all over each other, Big Muncey chuckling along with them, his boots well apart, his head nodding in acceptance of their reactions. That was Big Muncey. He knew how to play the game of charming people with vague references to himself.

Could he have had this effect on people if he had been short, skinny, and bald with a tenor voice? But he wouldn't be Big Muncey then, would he?

A year after high school, he could count on his close knit following of buddies. To their credit, they rarely drank beer or any of the local white-dog. They had learned how that would give them big problems at home and in their work. After their daily farm chores were completed, he and his assortment of friends had time to relax together and enjoy a little frog gigging or coon-hunting. Once a year they camped out for a weekend of fishing at Rough River Reservoir. Some Saturday nights they cruised nearby Bardstown and went to the Gypsy Drive-in where Big Muncey would watch the movie sitting on the hood of the car - in easy view of everyone.

His friends and he were not much interested in whatever lay beyond their known world - a territory of about ten miles in any direction from Chadwick. The world at large held no direct sway over them in their work and play.

By 1953, four of his following, who also worked on their fathers' farms, joined up with Big Muncey as a crew of bonded friends. They spent as much time together as possible. If one needed extra help, the others came to lend a hand. They could count on each other to assist on their fathers' farms. Before long, other nearby farmers began hiring them out as a team. During hay baling, farmers watched and marveled at the five of them. Also when setting tobacco, cutting it, housing it in the big barns, and later stripping it. As they worked together, Big Muncey and his crew kept up a stream of banter and teasing as they maintained a steady pace laboring shoulder to shoulder to get the job done. It was teamwork akin to playing basketball. Then, at the end of the day, they enjoyed their freedom until early the next morning. They knew to be ready for work at dawn. It was understood: "Keep them well fed, pay them fairly, and brag on them (but not too much)." The five of them - a farmer's dream crew of workers. While working or at play, the key, the catalyst was Big Muncey. The other four held him in awe.

Whenever the five of them were out cruising, girls noticed and flocked to them. Oh, the times those young men had! What about sex? Well, none of the other four would dare brave the embarrassment of going to the back of the town pharmacy and hanging around until the pharmacist, old Doc Threlkeld, finally noticed and came out and pulled open the special drawer containing Trojans. No one, that is, except Big Muncey. He would walk in boldly and ask Marge, up at the front register, for some "safes," and she, with a dark look, would lead him back to Doc Threlkeld. And later that night, whenever Big Muncey and his crew could find a field party or dig up some skanky gal at the drive-in, he would brag about not being scared of buying rubbers and would then produce a three-pack for each of them. He'd wink and sway a bit to left and right in a mixture of good humor and bravado and say,

"Damn if I can't find any cundrums big enough for me nohow. But I done got these little 'uns for you boys." Such brassy blarney they coveted.

Among his band of followers and workers, Willie Vaughn, more so than the others, allowed his life to revolve around his attachment to Big Muncey. Certainly Willie was regarded as no more nor less than the others. Although the shortest of the five, he could keep up with any of them at work and at play. His fascination by the Big Muncey persona, or, better, the enigma of him, soared so high that it seemed Willie sometimes forgot his own personality and identity. Vaguely suspecting this and its potential for harsh teasing from the others, Willie kept vigilant guard that they might not discern his dependence on Big Muncey.

Lattie, Willie's girlfriend, had long suspected that Willie spent far too much time talking about Big Muncey and marveling over him and his antics. One night, as they were parked behind The Baptist Church of Perpetual Responsibility, she pulled back from Willie and bluntly stated with the tone of repressed exasperation, "You know, Willie, sometimes you make me so mad the way you go on and on about Big Muncey. It's like you are living through him. *You're* my boyfriend, not him. He's no better than you, but when you brag about him it seems like you're putting yourself down. Why do you do this?"

Willie, after a brief struggle to keep his composure slowly replied, "You think I do? But now that I think on it, you're probly right. I'm not sure why, though. I like him. He's my friend. Has been all my life. Since first grade."

Willie paused for a moment, cleared his throat, and continued, "He makes me laugh. He holds us together. The five of us. You know how we work as a team. I really look up to him." He hoped that would satisfy her question.

Lattie moved away from him a few inches, breaking

their physical contact. He could tell she might be edging toward showing some jealousy, an emotion that he could neither understand nor endure. And if she started that stuff, the night was over. And, Lord above, this was Saturday night, their *special* night!

He took a breath, almost a sigh, and said, "You know, Lattie, the strangest thing happened day before yesterday. It started me thinking about what Big Muncey is really like. You know. Underneath. Remember how Mr. Cantwell used to have us read that literature stuff and dig into those characters in the story - about how who they really was was different from who they appeared to be? Well, something happened while we was rabbit hunting back down at the bottoms where Big Hole is. Just the five of us, as usual."

Lattie's lower jaw and lip jutted out, a conformation that did not appear in the least romantic to Willie. Her fingers were interlaced and not moving.

Willie forged ahead with his disclosure, "We was walking through the trees above the clearing, and Big Muncey pointed out a crow all by itself sitting on a high limb up in a sycamore. Sitting up there cawing, making all sorts of noise like it was daring us to go any further. Big Muncey grinned and said, 'Watch this!' He took and aimed his shotgun careful and winged that old crow on purpose. It tried to take off flying but just fluttered round and round to the ground squalling its head off all the way. It hit the ground and flopped around cawing. I looked at Big Muncey to see his reaction and to see if he did it for meanness or what. He just stood there like the rest of us watching, waiting to see what would happen. Just as Billy Earl was bringing his gun up to shoot it and put it out of its misery, several more crows appeared out of nowhere. And some more. And more. All of them cawing to beat the band. I bet'cha it wasn't more'n a minute when there was a hunnert of them black devils flying around, setting in the trees, swooping down to that wounded crow. Someone told Billy

Earl to hold off shooting. Them crows walked around that shot crow and tried to hep him up. They was acting like people trying to hep someone been hurt. Some of them in the trees was watching us and screaming like banshees at us. I saw more and more of them flying closer to where we was up there in the tree line. Some settling in the trees over our heads. I admit I got scared. Maybe they was gonna attack us."

Lattie shifted in her seat and glared at Willie. She blurted, "That poor crow. It wasn't hurtin' nobody. Big Muncey didn't have no right to shoot it."

By now, Willie was wide-eyed, confiding this frightening event. He continued, "You know them crows is about as big as a chicken. So I looked at Big Muncey to see what we was gonna do. And this is what amazed me. He was squatted down with his arms over his head scared to death. Done dropped his shotgun. He was actually scared. First time I ever seen him scared like that. He was looking up ogling his eyes to check on them crows flying in circles and landing in the trees above us. It looked liked most of them was circling up above the tree where Big Muncey was. Like maybe the hurt crow told on Big Muncey. I saw him hop up and he begun running bent over up the hill from tree to tree to get away. Course we done it too. I grabbed his gun and scooted up the hill behind him. Woods was a lot thicker up there. I figured if them birds was gonna attack us for revenge, I'd be safer in the underbrush. I admit I was scared half to death. Amazed. It was like them crows was black death gonna get us. We was all scared just like Big Muncey. After we got to the top of the hill, we made tracks for Joe Pat's barn. While we was running out in the open, I couldn't hear none of 'em close to us, thank God. Looked like they wasn't following us. They must a talked it over and decided to tend to that hurt crow. I figured it was their king or something. When we got inside the barn, Big Muncey's eyes was bugged out and he was mumbling about crows being messengers of the devil. I don't think that stuff with the crows bothered me as much as seeing Big Muncey acting like that. Scared like."

Lattie had scooted a little farther away from Willie, leaning a bit forward and looking at him as if he were a stranger to her. She murmured, "I always wondered about Big Muncey. And now, him ascared of some old crows?"

"Later, he just laughed like he does and told us that he wasn't frightened at all. Just wanted to scare us a little. When I started talking more about the way them crows come and circled, he said, 'Let's just drop it.'"

Lattie made a little "humpf" sound of "Well then." She shifted in her seat like she was ready for Willie to take her home. But Willie had a little more to tell.

"We didn't get together yesterday cause of the rain, but I drove by today to deliver some of Mom's canned tomatoes to Mrs. Campbell, and she told me Big Muncey was in bed with the flu. I was gonna ask her if I could go up to his room to see him, but her hall phone rang just then. I kinda stepped aways while she answered it, and what she said is what really surprised me. She was talking to Margie's mom. And Mrs. Campbell got an angry look on her face and said kinda loud and angry like, "Well, Edmund ain't gonna marry Margaret and that's settled."

Lettie's body jerked in her seat. Both of them quiet. The implication was clear: Big Muncey and Margie had cheated with each other - Margie had betrayed her boyfriend, Charlie, and Big Muncey had cheated on his own girlfriend, Ruth. Margie would probably have to go on a trip for a long time. Lettie finally spoke, "I can't believe they was that dumb. What a mess. And besides, ain't Margie the girlfriend of one of Big Muncey's best buddies, Charlie. One of those guys you work with and thinks Big Muncey hung the moon also?"

A Country Passing

This tale is in the dialect of old folks from the Chaplin, KY, area that I have studied beginning back in 1960. It amounts to a linear short story with a single point of view. The customs surrounding a death in a rural neighborhood have resulted in some fascinating research on my part.

In the old days
a death
required neighbors
and strict ritual
for laying out
a dear one
acorpse

A Country Passing

This very morning' Jancy, my old woman, heard the cowhorn from over Miss Maudie's way and come to the well I 'as adiggin'. Her voice squallin' down to me. Sky jest a round blindin' hole up above, and my Jancy's head lookin' down at me.

"Hit's not Miz Maudie ablowing thet cowhorn, Bayrin. Some-un' younger with lots of air. I reckon she's passed on. We better git on over an hep out. Do ar duty."

I spit out the rock dust and clumb up. Let my eyes accustom to the daylight. Hit done took cloudy an' still an' misty.

Jancy went on into old Miz Maudie's house while I tended to the horse and buggy. Over her shoulder, she sez, "You stay out chere with Ollie and Bud. Leave us to take care ah things inside. We'll call if we need you'ns."

I unhitched old Fanny and turned her aloose in the lot with the other horses. They ears pointy. Sniffing and laying back them ears. Circling. Whickering. Working out who's boss horse.

Bud and Ollie was in the driveway of the barn out of the damp alookin' at me. Faces set lak a glaring' of barn cats. I knowed fer sure then old Miz Maudie's done passed on. We'd be out chere til the women got her corpse ready fer the wake. Laid out on the cooling board.

Ollie and Bud and I sez howdy and nodded. No teasing this day.

Bud, he sez, "I done taken down the side door to her front room and put it crost two sturdy cheers. Then they run me out."

Ollie, he sez, "When Mag and I got here, she sent me

out to the springhouse fer water and some ah her canned corn and greenbeans and 'maters. Couldn't pay me a dime to get in the way ah them wimmen while Miz Maudie alaying there acorpse."

I sez, "Where we 'posed to dig 'er grave. Anybody been up to her fambly restin' place?"

Ollie, he sez, "I ain't diggin' no spadeful till them wimmen find the spot and tell me to." And we commenced to doing some serious tooth-sucking till Bud, he pulled out his bottle and offered it. They was a horse-fly settled on my knee knitting its legs. Side by side leaning our backs agin the stable boards we was settled back awaitin' turns fer a nip. Ready as rabbits, we were.

"Bayrin, come up to the house," I heared my woman calling fer me. My life ain't my own, seems. "Go fetch a ham from her smoke house. And git more water from the spring. An git that look offen yer face. No mully grubbs outen you this day."

During hog-killin' we put Miz Maudie's meat up fer her an' sich an' sich other chores. Old wider-woman.

I asted my Jancy how things was goin' inside.

"You jest stay outta ar ways. Nuthin' you needs to know." Her eyeballs all squinched up and kindly lak barkin' at me, she wuz.

But I know. They ascrubbin' her corpse and fixin' her up to put on the coolin' board. No fit place fir men folks. A candle along side. Some flai'rs in her hair. Pitcher of her old man and son nest to 'er. Ever little thang jest so lak they aspect of decent folks 'rounst about chere."

When I come to the back door with the ham, Jancy's arm come out an' taken aholt o' the wire on the shank. Not lookin' at me. Then she come back an' barked fer the water. Lips in a bunch lak she bitten into a green persimmon. No hi-dy-do, kiss my ass. No nothin'.

Up at the house, I could see them women with candles movin' round. Thet little bottle Bud brung done run dry fast. Me and the other men, glad he brung it, was feelin' a bit perkier. But we was careful to behave. I listened to the rustlin' of mice from the corn crib. Ollie, he tole about burnin' his plant bed an' deer tramplin' his garden. Bud, he lookin' off at the lane. We heard one of the horses break wind. Ollie, he smiled and lifted over and cut one too. Bud, he say, "Damn, Ollie. You worser then a jack-leg boy." So I tilted and let loose with a long growler an' looked up and seen the horses starin' at us over the gate.

More neighbors from our little community come by. We men stood around with ar hats on ar heads. Talkin' soft. One of the women stepped outen the back door and rang the big bell. We tramped up to the side porch and taken off ar hats and got quiet. Ollie's gubbertushed* woman tole us to go 'round to the front door. She met us there and opened up the door and let us in. One by one. There in the parlor was old Miz Maudie pretty as can be. Awearing her weddin' dress and lillies of the valley in her hair. She restin' on her white table cloth coverin' the coolin' board. The room quiet-lak, aways back from the chattering in the hallway. I took my turn and held my hat and looked at her. Seen where they was already several notes all tidy folded in the casket with her. Nodded my respect and walked back to where the big table was all set and loaded with food. Pulled out the chir nest to Bud and we took and begun eating while the women kept a watch over us.

Tomorrow, early, Bud and Ollie and me'll go up and dig the hole. Sam will say a few words and her homeplace'll be empty till the jedge he decides whut to do with it. Hear tell she got a niece over to Danville. Probly have the church funeral in six months. Big crowd. Dress up. Dinner on the grounds.

*bucktoothed

Intimacy and the Token

Not much fiction here in this linear short story with a single point of view. The central focus is intimacy, what is it and where can it be observed and felt.

For some
many perhaps
the concept of intimacy
is nil
but you and I
we are painfully sure
it is a part of us
in all places
and for all times

Intimacy and the Token

Today I awarded Harry, the man I sponsor, his eighteen year AA token. He had amassed three DUI's that many years earlier, and the poor guy plummeted, hitting a brutal bottom, losing everything: his family, home, job, license, car, and self-respect. Harry even did some jail time, and, struggling, became determined to rebuild his life.

Back then he asked me to be his sponsor, and I drove him to dozens of AA meetings and sat in on most of them. Some were closed meetings, but they let me attend, too, because I was an active participant in Overeaters Anonymous, also a Twelve Step Program. I loved being at Harry's AA meetings - its members raw, exposed, denuded, and struggling with sobriety the same as I was with food. As time passed, he worked through the AA steps and, bit by bit, entered a new life - without alcohol. Let there be absolutely no doubt, Harry is heroic in my eyes. Being his sponsor has been a fortifying experience for me, too. It works in both directions.

Each year I try to create a special event to surround the giving of the token to him, and I invite someone else, an unexpected person, to make the presentation. For a few days, I carry the token in my shirt pocket next to my heart, keeping it warm. When it is placed in Harry's hand, it bears my warmth along with the warmth of the person I've asked to award it. Throughout our private ceremony, we have tears, the three of us. Not floods, but enough for me to remove my glasses and dig out my handkerchief.

So, this year I took Harry to a restaurant on Bardstown Road, and we ordered salads. Bonded friends for years now, he and I sat there discussing the bones of sobriety and instances of important growth that had transpired in our lives over these years. We are not much alike - if at all. I live pretty much inside myself, and he is all over the place. So, as we have done often, our conversation centered on the idea of intimacy from our polar perspectives. *Intimacy* - I offer that it is a convenient word for the measure of loving relationships, yet neither of us, still, has become wise enough to capture and express all of its qualities. Only recently had we realized that having an intimate and loving relationship with oneself is also required for any recovery from addictions.

At the table, the two of us shared stories of our different relationships, those that appeared long-lasting and genuine and others that crumbled or became co-dependent and toxic early on. He had been sexually active, even promiscuous, most of his life, and, he concluded, hardly any of it had been intimate - merely casual and quickly forgotten. I had rarely had any horizontal relationships - thanks to my horrid formative years and a tragic marriage.

Yet, it came to my mind, I had been cloaked in a different, real sort of intimacy in my classrooms - with my pupils of all ages. Our vibrant bonding while we learned together and shared and explored and brushed shoulders and smiled, reaching out and realizing we were momentarily becoming a part of each other in sharing our lives every class period.

So, there Harry and I were in that fancy-schmancy restaurant sitting opposite from each other at a table with linen and a small carnation in a slender, crystal vase. At a nearby table were two ladies, both at least in their late seventies. The one with fierce black eyebrows was shaped like a turnip, her thunder butt lapping over the edges of her chair. The other could portray Popeye's beloved Olive Oyl - small head and long bones. Hands as big as mine. Both women wearing trophy rings with sumptuous diamonds. It only took one look, and I decided that each probably had been a glittering debutante way back - their manner, without question, blaring out the pampered and arch looks of the self-referenced wealthy, sitting there casually chatting and slowly sipping their cocktails - a cherry plopped into each. I love to study people. Especially those, like these two, who have their lives in headlines all over them.

Harry excused himself and went to pee, and, just before he returned, the big one leaned a bit closer to the bony one and stated, softly but firmly, with amusement in her voice, enough, though, for me to hear, "You blue-eyed slut." Not words I'd expect to over-hear out of two regal old gals. I wondered what prompted such a charge. Obviously, it also occurred to me, neither had been taken in by long years of Calvinism. It left me trying not to imagine Olive's abnormally long legs up in the air grinding away in wild debauchery. Probably they had been friends for generations and had seen the dispatch of several husbands.

"You blue-eyed slut!" - the long tall one apparently thought the comment was a few steps higher up than merely amusing, but she refrained from croaking out some feigned and shocked disclaimer. Merely allowed her face to transform into an open smile toward her companion, the type when a dear friend calls you a "son of a bitch" as a compliment.

With amazement, I realized I had witnessed another delightful form of intimacy. I pulled back from sudden laughter while the two of them paused, ignoring me, and examined each other's face for reactions. There, for a moment, was a scene from a stage comedy when the actors go into slow-motion while the audience calms down from rolling laughter, and they themselves do ordinary things with their hands and eyes and faces, one even reaching down to brush a crumb off a shoe.

Harry returned and we finished our salads in quiet friendship, the ladies at the other table paying no attention to us or anyone else, I noticed. Our waitress was nice and a hard worker. Probably had escaped a bastard of a husband or two, I supposed. Suzanne, her name. When she brought the bill in that black fold-over server's wallet, I asked, "Would you do something else? Harry here is an alcoholic and has been sober for eighteen years. Would you take this token from my hand and hold it in yours for a moment to give it some of your warmth and then present it to him for me?"

At first our waitress's eyes looked inquiring, and then, off the cuff, she began a typical, hollow awards speech, carefully searching out each remark. Suzanne had barely uttered a few cursory comments when her words bloomed into a heartfelt presentation of the warm token as the power of that moment and what she was doing grew in her awareness. It was her eyes again. They ceased looking stage-worthy and compliant and moved into the land of genuine honesty and sincerity, even showing signs of moisture when she told him how impressed she was and realizing what hard work it must have been for him. This woman neither of us knew and would probably never see again, a fellow human with a life of her own, on equal terms, reaching out to another human. And, during the pause at the end of her words, Suzanne stepped closer to Harry, hesitated, and then withdrew from giving him a hug. Instead she patted Harry gently around his shoulders and neck. More like short, intimate caresses. I watched. Her hands seemed to glow with loveliness. Harry sat looking unfocused like a child suddenly caught up in unexpected praise. And there I was digging out my handkerchief again. A powerful moment, I was certain, for each of us.

As Suzanne departed with the black server's wallet and money, she awkwardly bumped into a chair at another table and knocked it over. Fumbling and apologizing to the air around her, she replaced it and puttered around for a moment with the silverware and napkins.

Harry sat watching this while holding the token

between his two palms, prayer-like, as he took in Suzanne's struggles. The three of us, and maybe including the two old ladies, cloaked in thoughts of intimacies.

Survival

This is a tribute to a friend who, in spite of all, has his life together and is surviving while others have failed and disappeared - the type of man who values his life and the lives of others, too, even while standing high up in a tree.

I stand in awe
of those
who survive
their childhoods
and find happiness
high in trees
in clear thinking
by living with love
in spite all

Survival

You know, my friend
some people act out
while others sigh and grieve
their lives away
and there are those
who make up tales
and live them
like me
a few stand staring
hungering for
what's on the other side
plenty of folks
squat surrounded by stuff
lots of it
but people like you
climb trees
and others cut them down
I greet those who feel and wonder
like you
and move away from those
who won't and can't
who believe all sorts of junk
while individuals like you think and know
able to hug back and love
there are survivors
like you
like you
my friend

Uncle Elmon

This short story is mostly fiction, though I admit to thinking somewhat of my own Uncle Herman and Aunt Em. There came a time when I took Uncle Herman to say good-bye to his life-long friend, Jack. And it was cloaked in dignity and reserve - their formality with words, yet they innocently held hands. This story, too, is linear with a single point of view.

A family
in its many variations
and equations
drums along
with a quiet love
as the younger ones
help the elders
greet their endings

Uncle Elmon

Audrey's Uncle Elmon and Aunt Emma didn't have children, so Audrey, their only niece, though a bit of a tom-boy, became their surrogate daughter. Certainly, she did not relinquish being her parents' daughter and sister to her brothers, whom she referred to as "my ugly brothers," but she basked in the dotage of her aunt and uncle. While Audrey was a youngster, they weren't the sort to spoil her outright by giving Audrey everything she set her eye on, nor did they attempt to manipulate her life when she began making her own decisions. They recognized early on that Audrey possessed an independent spirit. Skeet and trail riding on horseback seemed suited to her. And besides, when she was needled by questions about when she might settle down into a marriage like the other girls in her cotillion, she flat out pronounced, "I will not become a trophy wife or a cookie baker wearing pearls in a beautiful house waiting for my man to come home from earning the money."

It seemed to Audrey that her aunt and uncle enjoyed being with her as much as she cherished being with them. And she could not imagine clinging to them or using them for her own advancement while she prepared herself to be the only female attorney in Centertown. Certainly, a respected attorney at that. However, she would never deny her fortunate kinship to them. The three of them had settled into an easy stasis, a balance wherein she danced her part and they danced theirs.

Stewart, Judge Cesna's son, with whom she had climbed trees and had hunted for snakes in the creek, stopped by her office one afternoon. A quiet day inside and out. The town square seemed deserted. He asked, "How's old Uncle Elmon doing? And Professor Emma?"

"You know, Stewie, I'm the luckiest person in the world

to have my Aunt Emma and Uncle Elmon. Most days, if I have time to drop by, we sit back, relax, and talk with each other. I enjoy their tales and ideas, and they listen carefully to me. How many people have someone who will actually listen and care about what the other person has to say?"

Mr. Elmon Colwell and Dr. Emma Muir Colwell were well known and respected citizens. Sunday drivers out to see the beautiful homes of Centertown made sure to tour past the Colwell place, one of those large residences with columns, a semicircular driveway in front, and a gorgeous garden in back. Emma Colwell, Ph. D., taught botany. Visitors would gasp in delight at her roses. Inside the mansion, they kept a bedroom for Audrey, and after high school she lived with them more than with her own parents or anyone else.

Emma held the position as professor at the college on the hill in Centertown, and Elmon ran a small but highly successful business on the square in town. For many years local folks recognized it as the sort of establishment that maintained a faithful clientele. A sporting goods store and place where seasoned house painters bought their paint. A comfortable place of first name recognition, high quality merchandise, and loyal clients who went back several generations.

Uncle Elmon took pride in his success and displayed it with his attire. Always a sharp dresser, fashionable, and natty. He liked to wear brighter colors when other businessmen wore black or drab colors. Audrey's uncle positively sparkled when he walked to nearby businesses along the town square. As he went from his store to the bank or to the drug store for a cup of coffee with a group of other businessmen, he began the short trek with business-like steps that eased into a friendly shamble as he recognized and greeted others on the sidewalks. During the waning years of the twentieth century, when other men relaxed their standards of attire and rarely wore suits, Uncle Elmon continued to stand out with his grooming.

The time and expense he spent in dressing better than ordinary folks trumpeted his attainment from starting out as a poor country boy who grew up on a tenant farm to becoming a well known and successful businessman with an elegant and brilliant wife. He never lost sight of his unsophisticated origins. Elmon had a way of greeting people, perhaps aquired after years in sales, an approach toward them with a twinkling smile and bobbing his upper body forward and back, almost, but not quite, in a courtly bow.

Over many years, Emma and Elmon Colwell had turned eyes wherever they went.

As Audrey chatted with her assistant one day, he remarked to her about how well dressed her uncle always appeared. She chuckled and said, "I helped him organize his walk-in closet one time and counted over fifty suits, numerous blazers and sports jackets, three tuxes, dozens of pairs of shoes, and a history of ties dating back to the Jazz Age, over seventy years. But, you know, Aunt Emma isn't that interested in clothing. She thinks it's pretentious. I think her attire is remarkable for its fabrics, subtle beauty, richness of colors, and that undefined quality some call style or good taste. But her closet is nowhere near as full as his. Somehow, it's her eyes that capture me. Their darkness and wisdom. They capture you with their brilliancy."

Audrey's assistant added, "It seems like to me that old folks place more value in their appearances than we do today."

She mused over that, laughed, and said, "Obviously, looking at us. No pearls or lacquered hair for me. Or heavy perfumes. Just neat and no rumples."

When Audrey announced that she had bought a condo further out of Centertown, Uncle Elmon looked at her with a mixture of pride for her accomplishments and with a touch of trepidation that she might fade away from them. It was in his voice when he spoke to her. Deliberate, low, and paternal. Assured that she would take in every word. He raised his bushy eyebrows when he faced her, and she settled her eyes onto his and avoided looking at his crooked nose, broken when he was a boy and had fallen from a birch tree. He said, "Audrey, I have always admired you for being your own person, and I hope you will keep in mind that you are always welcome to stay here with us when it suits you." And she continued to from time to time.

After Aunt Emma died, Audrey spent more and more time with Uncle Elmon. Now eighty-eight and forming cataracts, the day arrived when Audrey came by to take him out for supper. She noted that a front fender of his Cadillac was badly crumpled. The fourth time this had happened, and each time he had misjudged the rock wall near the entrance to his own driveway. She looked at him in his big chair, checking to see if he had any bruises or damage. He rose stiffly, gave her a look of resignation and, without a word, handed her his keys. She had his car towed away to be sold the next day.

Audrey decided it would be better to stay at the Colwell house, with her uncle, at night. Around this time, bad news arrived about Uncle Elmon's life-long friend, Judge Daniel J. Cesna. His son, Stewart, called her at work. "Audrey, this is Stewart. I'll make this quick. You know that Dad has been in failing health for some time. He and your uncle haven't played golf together for over a month now. Doctor Rue says Dad can only last a few more days. I wonder if you could bring Uncle Elmon by to see him. Dad asked me to check with you. I guess he knows the time is near, and he doesn't want to go without a chance to say goodbye. Those two have been friends all their lives."

Audrey sat back and thought: How will I handle telling

Uncle Elmon such disturbing news, and how will he react? How does one say goodbye to a friend of over eighty years, a steadfast friend who has survived a common history? Close as brothers.

By this time, Audrey had hired a sitter to be with Uncle Elmon each day while she toiled at her office or in court. And each evening, after a few moments afforded to herself, she would take him out to various restaurants for supper. That became their time to be together and for him to sparkle and be recognized by the public. Indeed, folks did treat him as local royalty. The staffs in each restaurant warmly greeted and pampered them. And often other customers came by their table for polite chats throughout the meal. They noticed how his niece tactfully helped him with names and mutual recollections and events. Audrey thought: This is not just my duty to Uncle Elmon. I find vicarious joy from the energy he derives from it. It seems that recognition and heaping on of praise are his personal validation and the strength behind his day-to-day living. He certainly enjoys talking about himself and his rise from poverty.

Often he chuckled to Audrey when she chided him for talking about himself so much, "Well, I'm the most interesting person I know." She smiled to herself and thought: It's not that he has no humility, but he certainly isn't weighted down by it. Not in the least.

Knowing that the judge was about to die, Audrey knew she had to tell Uncle Elmon. While driving back from a restaurant that evening, during the flow of pleasantries about the meal and whom they had seen, or rather who had seen them, she inserted that Judge Cesna had become quite ill. Uncle Elmon became silent at this information. News that he, no doubt, had been trying to avoid thinking about. Audrey wondered if he saw the probable demise of his friend as a portent of his own.

After a few more blocks of silent travel, Uncle Elmon said in a different voice, with sounds less sure, higher, almost squeaky, "I suppose we ought to pay him a visit."

She waited a moment and then offered, "Let's drop by now while we're close by."

Rather quickly, faster than she expected, he said, "Yes. I think that would be a good idea, Audrey." He always called her Audrey, never Honey or Audie, the last which she refused ever to answer to. For a second while driving, there flashed across her mind that one time in court when an opposing attorney dared to refer to her as "our heroic defense attorney, Miss Audie Murphy." Infuriated but in careful control of her words and actions, Ms. Audrey Colwell, Attorney at Law, crucified him there in court. Before Judge Cesna, no less. No other lawyer had tried that since.

She parked the car in Judge Cesna's driveway. Uncle Elmon looked smaller sitting there in the passenger seat. By the side of the driveway honeysuckle bloomed and drifted in the air. The lights from the house and the quiet of early evening brought back memories to her. The joy of playing there on these stately grounds when the judge's son and Audrey were children. Hide and seek and tag as the evening darkened and the fireflies began sparking here and there. The grown-ups on the screened-in side porch talking quietly as the children screamed and romped. The smell of the judge's pipe and the chinkling of ice in their glasses. The quietness of late evening. Mrs. Cesna came out in her Hawaiian muu-muu and placed the sprinkler near her front yard flower bed. Audrey and Stewart stopped their game to watch the four arms of it come alive when Mrs. Cesna turned on the water. The magic as water and air hissed from it and the arms began to circle, gathered speed as they rotated and spurted lines of water that danced in obedient streams and reflected tiny diamonds in the lights from the house. The center sprays of water like elegant ballet dancers. Their game immediately transformed into water fun as they dared each other to run through the outer spirals of drops. The voices from the porch rose a little and then settled back into their own magic of evening comfort in the ears of the children.

The reverie ended quickly as Audrey walked around the car. She felt surprise to see that Uncle Elmon had remained seated without attempting to open his door. She realized the dread he must be feeling. The visit would not be easy. And why should it? Each man had climbed up from the simplest beginnings, had survived long lives, and had buried their wives. They had been little boys and grown men together and had bonded in a rare friendship few people can even fantasize about.

"Better give me your hand, Audrey," he requested.

Just as she closed the car door, Judge Cesna's housekeeper came to the entrance of the house and recognized them. The Colwells had known Juliette for years. She came out and politely walked by the other side of Uncle Elmon, being there in case he wanted to lean on her arm also. The trio slowly walked into the house, into the brightly lit foyer with its large chandelier and portraits and curved staircase. For a moment Audrey became lost in images accumulated over the years on entering this beautiful home through those grand doors - the sounds, the smells, the anticipation, the realization that she was accepted as an important person by this family as well as by her aunt and uncle.

Juliette, ever tactful, in her comforting voice, said, "Well, Mr. Colwell we're so glad you stopped by. The judge will be mighty glad to see you. He's had such a hard time here recently, and he tires pretty fast. But I'm sure he will ask me to dress him to come out for a short visit. You probably know he stays downstairs now. We fixed up his study so he won't have to manage the stairs anymore."

As they entered, Uncle Elmon cleared his throat and spoke with unexpected strength, "Thank you, Juliette."

She ushered them into the spacious living room. Elmon and Audrey sat together on the couch and chatted politely about some of the items in the room: the ancient clock that had been in the cabin of the Cesna grandparents when they settled as pioneers, a life-sized portrait of Mrs. Cesna with her favorite Scottie dog, the sleek black baby grand, and the ancient Kentucky Long Rifle over the mantel. From the back, from his study, came the muted sounds of the judge as he fussed in his weakened voice, "Of course I'll see Mr. Colwell. Get my suit on me with that blue tie, Juliette. I won't be seen like this."

After long waiting, when Audrey and Uncle Elmon had fallen into silence and were staring at the door to the judge's study, Juliette wheeled him in. One look at the judge and Audrey knew he would be dead very soon, probably within the week. Yellow and grayish skin. However, Juliette had dressed him in a fresh suit with the blue tie.

He wheezed, "Hello, Elbo. It's a pleasure to see you." Audrey questioned to herself: Elbo!? That must be the teasing name the judge called Elmon when they were boys taunting and vying with one another.

Clearing his voice, Elmon piped, "Well, Danny, I sure am glad we decided to drop in. I hope it's not an inconvenience." The eyes of each of them sparkled at their open use of nicknames. "Elbo" and "Danny." Hearing those pet names, both Juliette and Audrey looked at each other and smiled.

Audrey watched as Uncle Elmon stood and did his obsequious, bowing walk across the room to shake the judge's hand. Juliette had already rolled the judge next to a large stuffed chair and, with a slight touch to Uncle Elmon's elbow, indicated for him to take a seat next to the judge. Audrey watched the two of them in awe, remembering her uncle and the judge as they were when she was younger, when they were still vigorous and in their prime.

Uncle Elmon sat forward in the chair, and, with unabashed ease, ignoring both of the women, reached over and took the judge's hand in his and held it firmly. They grasped hands while looking uncomfortably into each others' faces. Neither of them would ever consider holding hands with another man. Their eyes more moist than usual. No tears, though. They sat there nodding in unison. An unspoken acknowledgement of reaching the end of a very long journey. Two old men in their sorrow.

The judge said, "I haven't gotten anyone to purchase my stock in the Country Club yet. Have any ideas?"

Elmon replied, "I have a young friend, the man and his wife who bought my store. They've been hinting to me that they would like to buy my stock when the time comes. I'll let them know you want to sell yours."

Audrey and Juliette, as if invisible, watched them sitting there, two men holding blotched and wrinkled hands, talking about death while not talking about death as they struggled with the pretense of continuing life. A flood of pictures swirled through Audrey's mind. Images of these precious old men over the past eighty-something years. Little boys being chased by wasps. Boys climbing birch trees and swinging down on the springy boughs together. Young men going off to war and returning to greet each other with quickening relief on first seeing the other alive. Men struggling to acquire education and business acumen. Best friends standing up for each other at their marriages. Entrepreneurs taking risks to make lots of money. The two of them playing golf at the country club at least once a week. Confidants sharing their secrets and hopes and prayers with each other. Two who had grown old and had helped bury each others' wives. Elbo and Danny. Now shyly reaching out for the gentle touch of death.

Eugene

This short story has two points of view, the narrator's and that of an interior character's. It is entirely fictional, though I have noticed that most rural towns have an eccentric who is butt ugly and is usually ostracized. Sometimes the person becomes a hermit. And, there more commonly is a person or two who forcefully present themselves as different and, therefore, to be avoided and observed only at a distance. I think of a guy with long hair and a beard back in the 1960's when that was not done. No, sir!

We clap our hands
while dancing
laughing
and cheering together
so much alike

We cast stones
at the different ones
who dare to stray
close to us

Eugene

How does one measure a life? Especially one like his? People here-abouts in Magnolia County make mention, with casual derision, of Eugene now and then. Eugene Sheeks. One might even catch sight of him walking along the side of the road. He is, without doubt, the strangest looking and oddest behaving person they ever saw.

His seventh grade teacher in Appleseed said that Gene topped the list of the most down-right ugly, unpredictable pupils she had ever had in class. That was the same year handsome Senator Kennedy was elected President. None of the other pupils wanted to sit near Gene. Not only his body odor repelled them, but also his antics, some of which he could control and others it seemed like he couldn't. One day he left his seat, walked to the open window and jumped out. Two stories to the ground. The class, horrified, rushed to the windows expecting to see a broken body. Gene was standing there grinning and waving back to them - completely unharmed. Another day, he pulled out his tiny prick and pissed on four girls before the teacher grabbed him and dragged him out of the room. He was already sixteen, so the Board of Education quickly met and expelled him. After that, Gene pretty much stayed at home with his parents. On Saturdays they would come to town to buy groceries and do a little shopping, his parents and Gene in their rattle-trap old farm truck. On return, Gene rode with the groceries in the truck bed watching the world go by - backwards.

On one occasion when he was eighteen, his mother got Gene to drive her to the little country store. They didn't allow him to drive often and never alone, not after he sideswiped the town cop's car. He loved driving, though, and usually behaved when he was given that privilege. No waving at people or stopping off at places. No beeping the horn or revving the engine at the town's only stop sign.

In the dank store, his mother gave her list to Miss Azbell, the grocery lady. Gene stood near the screen door watching, surveilling like an owl. Only his head turning. After Miss Azbell gathered the items and placed them in a box and had written up their ticket, Gene obediently carried the box out. Old Miss Azbell shook her head as she watched him leave with his mother. Mrs. Carlyle was in the short line of women waiting with their shopping lists and commented to Miss Azbell, her voice rather quiet, "That boy of Mrs. Sheeks is the strangest boy I ever did see. Looks funny. Acts funny. Talks funny. But he did hep his mamma just now. Look how he walks. Bowlegged so's a calf could run through and never touch a knee."

Miss Azbell gave a little snort and added, "He come in here last week, I think it was, and never looked up. Crooked teeth. Hair going ever-whicher-way. Big ears. If he got caught in a wind, it'd carry him off."

Beula Abshear, waiting her turn, had been listening and joined in, "I think if I'd a birthed that boy, I'd a never a let 'im out the house. He started out plum ugly and he gotten worser. The least she could do is keep him home and out of sight."

This was too good for Georgia Girvin, standing behind Beula, to miss out on, so she decided to add her two cents. "I wouldn't let my boys play with him cause he jest looked wormy. That lil' bit of a nose always hangin' green snot. Them pig eyes won't hardly hold a look. And stink! Lordy, that woman musta never learnt him to take a bath! He walks 'round with his eyes all skrinched up and one lip adroopin' and the other'n pulled up like a mare gittin' serviced."

By now, the women were chuckling along with one another in good fun, secure in knowing they weren't that ugly and that their children weren't either. Each of them swung their heads for a quick additional peek at the boy as he carried the groceries to the truck. These town ladies who together seemed as powerful as a commando unit.

At the end of the day, as Miss Azbell was closing up, she remembered Gene and the amusement she and the others had in describing him. She recalled the first time when Mrs. Sheeks, that poor woman, had brought him into the store. A week old. The other ladies in the store stopped what they were doing and rushed to inspect the new baby, and they cooed and said the expected words. But each thought: "For a moment there, I wasn't sure just what it was she was aholdin'." And each of them wordlessly imagined the thought common to formerly pregnant women, *What musta it been like for that poor woman while that baby was growing in her. Did she have any suspicions that it might turn out to be like that?*

Miss Azbell locked the front door of the store and began the short walk to her house on Carter Street. *Eugene Sheeks! What could he be like inside? Clothes mismatched jest like his body parts. Arms short. Fingers small and knobby, rough as sandpaper. Squeaky little voice when he does says somethin'. And that hind end he's got. Never ever seen one like that'n. Pokes out like two footballs turned sideways. Them eyes all sunk back in his head. Eyebrows bushy as a judge's. Him skittish as a rabbit. I've seen lots of folks around here whose heads seemed to be baked in a slow oven, but that poor ole boy, Eugene...*

Out Sally's Silo Road, a few months after moving there from Louisville and settling into his new A frame to write and meditate, the new man, Lowell, decided to drop by the Sheeks place to say hello. They had never come to him, so he decided to go to them. Figured he should become acquainted with his closest neighbors.

It was a memorable visit.

That night, Lowell wrote in his journal:

As I approached their humble board and batten house, I felt that flash of hesitation I always get just at the moment when I can no longer reverse myself.

Their boy, Gene, was slopping the pigs and saw me walking down the road. He dropped the bucket and ran for the house. Before I got to the steps, I heard their bell clanging from the post at the back of their house. Probably Gene calling for his father, I thought. Mrs. Sheeks came to the front door when I knocked. She was Suspicion personified. Gene was nowhere to be seen, but I could feel his presence nearby. Mrs. Sheeks narrowed her eyes at me and asked what I wanted as if I were some sort of derelict or drug crazed mass murderer. My beard and hair again, no doubt. I tried not to become unmindful of the probable simplicity of their lives and their isolation. She looked like a dried-apple doll, face all wrinkled and shrunk in. Hair pulled back in some sort of braided knot. Leaning toward her and offering my hand, I caught a whiff of waxy, sharp lemons and ammonia. Maybe she had just stopped cleaning with Mr. Clean and Pledge. I told her that I was her neighbor and just wanted to say hello. Her hand-shake was swift, and her fingers felt warm and bony like a bird's grip would be. She inspected me and obviously didn't like my long hair and beard, which are my pride and joy. I kept up an innocuous stream of chatter while she made little looks at me. If I had jumped, she would have run for a gun, no doubt. I heard a sound from the side of the house. I'm sure it was Gene lurking and listening. Maybe he stood ready to protect his mother in case this odd looking alien from outer space were to do harm.

Old Man Mr. Sheeks came steaming through the house like he had expected some emergency. He was a dead-ringer for a character right out of Steinbeck's "The Grapes of Wrath." Somewhat stooped and smelling pretty high, red faced and blowing air.

As I introduced myself, I held out my hand to shake. He hesitated then reached his hand out with a feeble dead-fish shake. Fingers only. Rough fingers with crud in the creases. He also gave me a long disapproving look. Neither one of them cracked a smile at anything I said.

Being a bit daring, probably, I asked Mr. Sheeks to tell his son to come on out from the side of the house - that I wanted to meet him, too. They both made a little jump and must have finally realized that I really was a neighbor and that they didn't want to seem backward and rude to me. He gave me the surly look of one who is being imposed upon.

Those two struggling people. Mr. Sheeks called out, "Oh, Gene-boy! Pull in your horns and come 'round here and meet our new neighbor. Come on, now!" There was a distinct manner in his words and body language throughout his calling Gene that reminded me of that type of men who thrive on setting another person up to be duped, to get one over on, to make the other person become lesser. The sort of man who would gyp his grandmother and then laugh about it.

I guess Gene was maybe eighteen then. Strangest looking kid I believe I've come across. My first impression of him was that he appeared to have just then been caught at some terrible crime and was steeling himself to hear a torrent of the vilest obscenities descend upon him. Before he went vacant eyed, he made a quick look at me, his eyes keen, and at the same time he pulled up his lower jaw and lips attempting to make a seal against his upper teeth, such as they were, all protruding and grayish and disorganized - at the same time attempting to slurp up an accumulation of spit. Whew! A really bad set of teeth.

That boy hedged around the corner of the house, stepped up on the porch and stood near his mother as cautiously as one walking through a mine field in Korea. His parents stood silent, so I introduced myself to him and held out my hand. The hand that came to mine felt like dry sticks, I swear, and jerky with fear. It took all of my control to keep my eyes on him as I spoke. Sort of like talking to a person whose face had been horribly burned. A face barely human any more. His upper lip was lifted from his mouth and teeth.

I asked him a few questions about school and sports and hunting and fishing. For most, he gave blank looks. Several times as we chatted, Gene reached up to squeeze a pimple on his cheek, rubbing the pus and blood on his trousers as if he were unaware of what his hands were doing.

I wondered if the boy were retarded by nature or by nurture?

I think he is an example of an unfortunate kid who is probably average or better in intelligence, but his looks trump that to everyone else, even his family. Standing there next to us, he rocked a little to his left and back in a pulsing motion as his sunken eyes darted from my shoes to a quick glance at my beard and hair and then to the road and back. I decided that Gene was caught up somewhere in a storm, and helpless. I knew that the storm consuming him was not the same as the one I swirled about in.

After I walked back to my place, I built a little fire in the fireplace just to watch the soft flickering of the flames and to think. This would be an important date in my life. An event as memorable as graduation or first getting laid. The Wednesday that I met the

Sheeks - that I first encountered Gene. Much of my early stories and poetry had been about my youth. About being a misbegotten child. And thinking about Gene, I made guesses about his life.

Now that I live here in rural Kentucky, closer to the earth, reality has become more readily defined and acceptable. I wondered about Gene and what kind of world view a boy like that might have.

As I sit here now before my fieldstone fireplace, the measurements of the room seem to be changing, becoming smaller and more intimate. Thinking about our differences, the Sheeks and mine, it comes clear to me that they belong here in this place because they, no doubt, have kin buried here. Thus, I will never, no matter what, actually belong here like they do. Even if my ashes are strewn somewhere here, I will remain an outsider - a damaged soldier who had a beard and long hair.

Even now, after all the experiences of my life, there are many questions in my mind that are too complex for my own understanding - bits and pieces of life that I have learned to pass over in silence hoping that I might understand them when I have lived more. Could Gene be grappling with similar questions of life? Might he also be a victim of a society that shoves different looking people aside. Like they have me. Have his needs for acceptance been rebuffed so many times that he rarely reaches out any more?

But in my case I choose to repel ordinary society. I could have a haircut and a shave and be accepted if I wanted to. But Gene?

I realize now that after Korea I backed away from most people and into the security of contemplation. Into books, music, and solitude. I shut out my people and the absurdities of their lives. For a while I rushed to have more, to compete more, to be a member of the "in" groups - but that was artificial and definitely not me. I had seen too much death and had killed too many - not knowing why. People had died in my arms all for a group of industrialists who controlled the government. We were soldiers, pawns led by men who were seeking higher ranks while we fought and died. We grunts had to obey orders from the high ranking officers who were safe. They gave the orders and lived it up, and we suffered and died. Majors and colonels and generals with maps. Big brass using our lives as they competed with each other for advancement in rank and to impress each other.

When I came back to the states, I watched as my country continued to ignore its entrenched absurdities and injustices. After a short time, I made it my job to reject my own nation. I didn't want to be with those who dressed alike and thought alike and cheered alike and wanted more and more. As I watched from the outside, became increasingly aware that most people were bobbing around in a sea of superstitions and myths, and they seemed to be searching for cracks and crannies to stuff in more. People rejecting reality for mumbo-jumbo beliefs. I would not be a part of that. And still won't.

I realize there are others like me. More and more of them. They buy my books. It enthralls me to write the stories others harbor inside themselves. I write about the absurdities of tribalistic values and the greed that define our times. My publisher sells my books to make money and has no interest in what the books say and mean. And I receive my share of the money they send me. I live in my own little hovel of hypocrisy.

Can a person live a minimalist life, a pristine life? Can I reject those people and remain alive? Where has our simplicity gone to? Maybe Gene is the better mystic and already knows the answers. Obviously he owns his life, and I do not.

The hearth fire having settled, Lowell put aside his journal.

Eugene is now in his forties, and he has a dog companion. An ugly, mottled mutt always at his side. And we, you and I, see him, see them. He is established thereabouts as a hermit who comes to town only when he must. He and the dog walk by the side of the road while cars and other vehicles whip past them. The modern world pressing hard against them. To the townspeople he seems to be taking refuge in another time. People see them and pity them. Yet, they wonder about Gene. What must it be like to be a hermit, an ugly troglodyte?

Word is that he still keeps the little place that his parents left him. Run down. Electricity off. No phone. Sometimes, in the night, carloads of teenagers drive by, and they scream and yell and toss their beer cans in his yard. His dog wuffs several times on alert, but it cowers close the Gene. He never comes out or waves a gun at the hecklers. This is the way of those young folks. Greedy of their own beauty and unaware of their poisonous acts. This is their refusal to countenance Gene's difference and repugnance. It is their rejection of a man who does not participate in the flow of their lives. A recluse who eschews their things and fads, their appearances and demands for more and better. It is a relief to them that they do not resemble him.

When their taunting becomes too worrisome for him, he and the dog head for the deep woods, to a place he considers a good natured lower heaven, where he can expand and not be seen, and he can hang onto the sounds of breezes and birds and leaves and water. Where he knows the languages of night woods and day life. Where the haunting looks from others become erased and their memories impotent. Where he basks in the loving eyes and comforting presence of his dog.

He camps for days, for weeks during warm weather. Sometimes when it is cold, too. Gene builds a lean-to. He lives off the land mostly. Fish, fowl, raccoons, possums, snakes. He has learned about herbs and wild plants that he can eat. He bathes in the same spring-fed stream that brings him clear clean water to drink. He hears the birds and the silence of trees and air and sky and stars. The man has staked out his territory there in the forest in the same manner of any other animal. He and his dog are a part of the fauna there.

On a night of a full autumn moon, Lowell, the writer, now long past his youth, thinks of Gene, imagining his life in the woods - a private time for the hermit. He envisions that Gene is in a glade, standing and watching to the east. The darkness and the stars. There is a glow in the black, clear sky, and the Milky Way comforts his eyes. He sees bulging up from the infinity of sky the top of the yellow moon setting fire to the horizon. As it rises, Gene removes his shoes, his clothes. He stands fully naked facing the moon. A man who no longer cries with his whole body. He turns and bows to the four directions, his body pale as a grub in the light of night. He bows to all that is the earth and the moon. An owl has begun calling. There is a whippoorwill singing out its eerie night music. Lowell, sitting in comfort in his snug A frame, plays the sounds in his mind as the night birds speak and Gene lifts his arms as if beseeching. Or is it in praise? There in the deep silence of the full moon.

To us, we envision two men, different from us. We, who are so blessed by our sameness and our belonging to one another. We observe an ugly man standing naked, glowing under the beauty of the full, magnetic moon - and an old writer comfortable at the side of his hearth, and he, too, is illumined -

by orange flickering lights. Both men seem in full contact with the power and beauty of the universe. Both unconcerned, now, by how others see them.

Little Imp

I love this little story-poem. It actually happened to me while driving down Helsinki Hill to New Haven, KY. Nothing else to say about it.

Have you walked
beside a highway
and become angry
at cars and people
speeding by
maybe offer
a finger
or yell
shit-head
just to balance things

Little Imp

He was a rural boy
happy as a flop-tongued
dog
in mid-summer exploration
maybe ten
with loose straw hair
no shirt
and wearing wet bib
overalls
barefoot
walking in the grass
alongside the road
near the bottom
of a speed downhill

Eyes wide
they caught mine
and in that instant
as I drove past him
there was pure delight
on his face
as he quick-tossed a snake
onto my windshield

A water snake
perhaps pounded to death
in the creek
by this crafty hunter

Its belly yellow
with a gray back
it bounced off to the road
twisting in flight

I lurched in my seat
of course
of course
quick slowed
and stopped

Looking back for the boy
now vanished
into the brush
hugging himself
no doubt
no doubt

and giggling with glee

Little Imp

Old Emmett

This short story is mostly fictional, though I admit there was an old gentleman who did sing out inappropriately in church where I played the little organ. It is single point of view, the narrator's voice in first person. Writing it, I felt the import of the demise of an old man who had been young and important to the community for years and years.

Somewhere along
his journey
he became an old foggy
and people ignored
his slow dying

The sort of man
whose antics
they ignored
remembering
his better days

Old Emmett

He was no longer a go-getter merchant or the envy of other men. Mr. Emmett Anderson had morphed into a thick, round, elderly man bothered not one whit by his public image. Nowadays, Mondays through Saturdays, he sat up front in his pocket-sized clothing store which was next to the drug store and a few steps from Burleigh's one flashing red light. Indeed, to call it a haberdashery would sound too highfalutin. By the time I came to Burleigh, the inside of the store seemed dim and musty to customers, rare then as they were, though there were large windows at the doorway and several single-bulb overhead fixtures, large bare incandescent lights dangling from the impressed tin ceiling. Counters laden with ordinary items of apparel, mostly for men and boys, lined the walls, and farther back, a rack of suits and trousers crowded the aisle. One side of the dressing room door, saloon type, remained open giving the false impression that a shopper had just stepped out to admire himself in the three triptych mirrors. Any curious children who wandered by or came into the store with parents immediately ran to the magic of those mirrors, to take a stance and gawk and turn and wave in wonder at themselves visible in rare three dimensions.

At the front of the store, Emmett, picking at an ear, kept watch beside the glass case containing articles that might accompany the purchase of clothing. There were wallets, tie-pens, studs, ties, belts, handkerchiefs, socks, underwear, and even shoelaces. On the first wall counter, handy for young rural men, was a large selection of blue jeans. He also had a small assortment of shoes for men, but anyone who wanted to purchase shoes from Mr. Anderson would bypass his collection and have him order a pair through the mail. Bear in mind that this was a humble, small-fry store in a quaint burg back in the 1960's when Louisville had only one mall, and to shop there meant a full day's trip back and forth. Most of the people of Burleigh and the surrounding area drove to Louisville or to Bardstown only if it were absolutely necessary.

By this time, Old Emmett Anderson usually sat at the front of his store and watched people passing by. Advanced age had come upon him too slowly for him to notice, and now he was bereft of any expected sense of indignity or nuance of courtesy. When he did speak to someone, the words were gruff and often seemed painted with outrage. That and his breath was rank and, at times, even fetid. These days none of the other town characters came in to loaf with him. Just looking at him, he seemed unfriendly with his glaring hog-like eyes and flabby face and bulbous nose - certainly more than a bit daft and unpredictable. When he had an idea or a topic worming around in his head, it could not be dislodged or subdued by any conversational give and take or decorum. He spoke his guts - loudly and with no notice of the listener's reaction. His language was not coarse, and his topics were never crude. Just wearisome and long-lasting until he drifted off into uncomfortable mumbling. Usually he was caught up on politics, politicians, world affairs, a tid-bit or two of local interest, or a dim recollection from the past that had evolved into an unrecognizable annoyance to him and needed to be aired.

It had been noticed that, with increased frequency, he would leave the store open and wander up and down the town's sidewalks nodding at people and seeming to be searching for something or someone. Most people tactfully faded out of his view or found alternate routes to wherever they were going. Those souls he did encounter and begin talking to, listened politely and shifted about in front of him until they realized, eventually, he was actually talking to himself - and they would walk away silently.

My first encounter with Mr. Anderson was in church, the Burleigh Presbyterian Church. Its building could accommodate up to fifty adults if they weren't too broad in the beam. Most Sundays, twenty to twenty-five worshippers attended. A student pastor and his wife lived in the manse next door. His sermons were formal exegeses prepared for his classes at the seminary where he was still a student. They had depth, wisdom, dignity, reason, history, and a heavy dose of shaming and guilt boiling up from the Calvinistic doctrine of original sin. As my tenure there progressed, the congregants seemed faithful in attendance for no reason that I could discover. Certainly, no one, as far as I could determine, was caught up in exploring personal existential credos or was passionate about the life and teachings of Christ, preferring the horrors of the Old Testament instead.

Fresh from college, when I moved to Burleigh to teach Latin at the high school, word soon reached the youthful minister that I could play the piano - therefore, "that man ought to be able to play the organ," they, the *vox populi*, decided. Thus, since word had also been passed along that I claimed to be Presbyterian, he drafted me to play the organ for the Sunday services. On several other occasions in larger communities, I had played huge, courtly pipe organs and had been thrilled by their power and sounds. They made Baroque music sound Baroque, and Bach was my favorite. If I were to provide Sunday music for the church here, they would not hear popular music. Cutesy tunes for the untrained would never flow from my fingers and feet.

Needing to try out the organ, I drove to the small church. To my disappointment, it was a pip-squeak electric one with two partial manuals (keyboards) and an octave of pedal notes below. The selection of stops was no more than eight. Not much for making great organ sounds. To fish up real music from this alleged King of Musical Instruments would be a challenge. At its best, it could not escape that tinny electronic timbre one expects to hear in a single parlor funeral home from a similar gadget tucked away out of sight from the mourners. So, being Presbyterian (at the time), I decided to make do as best I could with what I had. The minister and his wife picked out the hymns for each service, and I picked out music for the meditation at the opening of the service, the offertory, and the postlude. With rare exception, I played from Bach's *Well-Tempered Clavier*, his timeless preludes and fugues.

And you have to know about this: Since the organ was electric, I quickly found out that it also picked up any nearby CB transmissions from anyone driving up the hill outside the church. One memorable transmission came from the driver of a local wrecker. As the worship service cycled along, during a pause we heard through the organ's speakers, loudly and clearly: "Tell him I'm on my way, god-dammit." It echoed around the room and bounced defiantly off the stained glass windows. I jerked upright on the organ bench. No one else showed any sign of hearing anything. Not even a gasp or a giggle. My head sputtered at this. Maybe these people accepted other discomforts without responses - a congregation accustomed to showing rare valor in times of need.

In the loft with me and The Squeaky Organ were five or six people in sedate robes - The Choir, including Mr. Emmett Anderson. Emmett was sucking on a peppermint, and the others wore various perfumes or after-shave lotions. They were local folks and had known each other all their lives. Their people had lived in this area for generations. They attended this church just as their ancestors had done. Very nice people. Patient with me and curious about any new person, a man, an outsider who taught school and was proficient in playing the piano and organ. "A man musician!" Certainly an oddity, it seemed. Word was that there was one other man from that area who knew how to play a piano, and he moved away. I suspected he may have fled for his own safety from badgering community expectations to accompany all of their programs, weddings, funerals, and even those wonderful small community fundraisers called "PTA Womanless Weddings" when local macho men were dressed in wedding drag and hammed it up to a roaring crowd.

In that choir loft is where Mr. Emmett Anderson became a part of my life, however briefly. He sat near me, on my left. When I looked over to him, I felt a clear sense that I was a defective in his beady, hog-like eyes as he tongued his peppermint.

During the very first Sunday there, for the prelude I played "Sheep May Safely Graze." It went smoothly. As soon as the minister stood, I gave the intro chord for the doxology, and the little choir rose to begin singing - all but Emmett, who was occupied with thumbing through the Order of Service bulletin. Half way through the doxology, he lifted his chin and began singing the first hymn loudly ("Abide with Me") and, with firm intent, belted it out regardless of what we were doing. So before the choir and I had finished the doxology, old Emmett Anderson had struggled to his feet and was braying away with wrong notes and questionable tempos until he must have decided he was finished - and then sat down. I looked around the choir and the congregation for their reactions, and no one met my eyes. Everyone sat relaxed, tranquil, and expectant just as if the course of the service was roses and light. I looked at Mrs. Anderson, his wife, seated on the front row wrapped in a ratty mink stole, and she, meeting my eyes, just barely moved her head less than an inch either way with the patience of one who knows suffering. I had the distinct impression that she was tolerant of him, inured, perhaps - that of her married life with him, every year a new layer had been added, this most recent one the most demanding of all.

Mrs. Anderson was a study herself. Not at all one of those irksome women with blue hair and a fixed smile. I later discovered her name was Viola. She was thin on top and as plump as a gourd below. That mink stole was a mantle of majesty around her, at least in my eyes. I wondered about her life with him, with Emmett. If she knew what she was getting when she agreed to marry him. Did he bull his way around with a sense of prerogative even then?

Each time we sang, Mr. Anderson repeated his performance - with undiminished fervor and entitlement. When we sang "Holy, Holy, Holy," he sang the doxology and a bit of "Little Brown Church In the Valley." When we eventually finished the last verse, he was still going strong. The body language of the small congregation and the choir and the minister bespoke nothing of any amusement they were experiencing or that anything was out of the ordinary - only the fraudulence that must have been indigenous to their gathering. But hysterical laughter was wrenching away inside me. My breathing had become ragged, sharp little snorts as I struggled not to disgrace myself.

Later, when I captured the young minister, I asked him about Mr. Anderson. As if I had stumbled upon some small disorder in a peaceful world, he offered dismissively, "Oh, yes. That's just Old Emmett."

Old Emmett was the case of a great bull elephant clumping and trumpeting through a room and nobody showing any notice much less alarm or hysterical laughter. The local folks apparently denied his existence throughout that time of his mental demise. He attended church only a few more months, and then he vanished from my view. I imagined his skin growing patches of thin moss while he approached his death. I must be honest in admitting his physical departure made my life at the organ much, much easier and less strangled with repressed laughter. The words from Tennyson, *"I am a part of all I have met..."* came to me like thunder. No doubt Mr. Emmett Anderson had been a part of my life, and I must have also been a part of his at least in some vague way during those months of his decline. I hadn't heard that he had died, so, I supposed his family must have begun keeping him at home. I noticed a "Closed" sign at the door of his store, and the church services continued without him just as they had with him.

Later, a month or so, his wife, Viola, phoned asking me to play some sweet but soothing music for his funeral. Of course, I agreed, and gritting my teeth, I dragged out some evangelical music from one of the other churches to play quietly in the background on the equally gritty little organ at the funeral home - way back in another room, thankfully. But during the service I thought of Old Emmett, the man he had been years ago when he was an important cog among the merchants of the town, a person of moment and reach, and an elder in the church. A respected gentleman. I imagined how people would drop by to chat with him and then share his wisdom with others. How he could tell a great joke and then laugh from his toes up, even his bones filled with sounds loud enough to be heard clearly in the drug store and across the street. I know those thoughts of Emmett will remain in the lives of the inhabitants of Burleigh for generations. And they will politely omit any mention of those awful years of his decline.

The Hazards of Reading

Emily said it better:
"no frigate
like a book"

The Hazards of Reading

Like standing nude in moonlight
under her capture
reading erases my self
and takes me anywhere
everywhere
trips beyond my tribe
and its captors
who grasp at me
to protect me
from the lunacy
of others
in books

And like stretching
exposed under the sun
lit up by his heated force
the air heavy with summer sultor
insects clattering
I become the words
that sculpt interiors of others
the troubled ones
the laughing twos
threes in love
survivors
and characters
who have sprung
from higher minds

In books
I dare to rise
to face my brother the sun
my sister the moon

Yea, Though I Walk

This short story is partly fiction in the first person point of view. It takes place in a condominium building and is presented in counterpoint to the earlier story, "A Country Passing," and it illuminates the differences between dealing with a neighbor's death a century ago and now.

Yea, Though I Walk

Frantic banging and the ding-dong bell at my condo door. Just as the evening news began.

"Coming!"

Was it a former pupil? Some late-running UPS person with a package?

"Michael! We've knocked and called and Mrs. Shuler's newspaper is still at her door and her car hasn't been moved all day!" Two of my condo neighbors. Their voices high and jumpy. Janice, a young woman, a refugee from Katrina - and Darla, a burly androgen from down the hall.

For several years now, at old Mrs. Barbara Shuler's request, I had kept her door key. "Just in case," her voice had trembled. I had long been her appointed "would-you-take-out-my-garbage-please" neighbor. Mondays and Fridays.

The faces of the two, of Darla and Janice - masks of fear and helplessness. From me, "I've got her key here!" Grabbing for the antique milk pitcher where I keep assorted keys and locks. Quick digging around for Barbara's door key tagged with a white plastic heart.

Then, the three of us stumbling into each other down the hall to her door. I knocked loudly. "Barbara! Barbara! We're coming in!"

Pushing inside Barbara's elegant condo, we jerked at an unfamiliar smell. I went to the right into her little sitting room, and the other two to her bathroom and bedroom. On her couch lay the crossword puzzle and pencil. Unfinished. No Barbara, the bent old lady. From the bedroom door, Janice's loud voice, "She's on the floor! Not moving!"

Janice's panicked voice. "911! Call 911!"

I made my feet work - to carry me into the bedroom. A

strong smell of shit and puke. In the dimness, Barbara's feet and bare legs. The old lady unmoving and prone on the floor, face down, wedged in the space between her bed and the window. Her ashen form in the dim room - and the intrusion of seeing her plump derriere and sensible old lady panties. A tangled sheet around her chest. I, who had worked in an emergency room, leaned down and touched her shoulder. Cold. Lifted her arm. Rigid. From that jostling of her body, I heard the post mortem grue of a burp gurgle from her. "She's dead. Cold. Rigor mortis." Darla stepped closer, leaning over for a verifying look at Mrs. Shuler. Nodded her agreement. We left the room. To the big room. Throughout, a thought drummed in my head: What did she think in her last moments?

Janice on the phone, "No. We're sure she's dead. She's just an old lady and hasn't been well. Her newspaper.... Police are on their way? What about EMS?"

A policeman came and casually walked into the bedroom while we babbled on as if we had been educated by Rhesus monkeys. He emerged breathing through his mouth and took a seat at her dining room table. Roly-poly sort of fellow. Used his police radio to pass along there was no hurry for the EMS. Started writing notes paying little attention to us. "Who's her next of kin?" he asked.

None of us knew. So, Janice, Darla, and I began poking around, opening drawers, looking through papers, searching for her address book or anything that might list an emergency contact person.

In walked a handsome man. No, a woman. The EMS person. Chiseled features. Sleek black hair combed back in a ducktail. She and Darla leaped for each other. Into a strong football player hug. And a tight-lipped kiss. The policeman, shaking his head, returned to his note taking. We talked over each other telling the medic what we knew, and she broke loose from Darla and walked heavily into the bedroom, came out and began chatting with Darla about Pride Week and the Gay Pride Festival down at the river. Janice and I got busy again searching for Barbara's address book.

The coroner arrived. A man. Perfect teeth. Friendly. Hair I instantly envied. His right side fully functional. His left side... leg in a brace. Maybe a prosthetic leg. His left butt meloning out much bigger than the right. His left hand and arm as unmanaged as a leafless branch caught in strong, gusty winds. He lurched toward the bedroom snapping on the gloves, not an easy task with his left arm shooting out disobediently in all directions. The policeman kept at his note taking, and the EMS person followed the coroner into the bedroom. After a minute or two, out they came chattering - with Mrs. Shuler's wallet. And her emergency contact information. Of course, I realized, she would keep her purse and wallet close to her bed at night. Old lady. We hadn't thought to look in there. Into the death room.

The coroner bragged over Mrs. Shuler's emergency card. "She's got all her meds and names and phone numbers right here. I'm supposed to call her lawyer."

We had stopped our chatter to listen to him. Waiting to hear what he would do. Then his cell phone rang. Some lengthy discussion about another death. A baby. One day old. And another call about a human-looking bone someone found in the West End. He glared at us and began grumping about not being able to be in three places at once.

We eyed each other - Mrs. Shuler's neighbors - curious about the same thing. Her possessions. Especially her jewelry. And each of us now a dedicated guardian of Mrs. Shuler's keepsakes and treasures. She was a part of us - our condo-mate. "Where are her rings? Is she wearing any?" I dared to ask.

In moments, the three women were in her kitchen looking through her meds and cabinets. I inspected her writing desk and its drawers. No sign of a cache of jewelry anywhere. Maybe she had anticipated her demise and her neighbors digging around for her precious possessions. And maybe they were in a safety-deposit box. I would never find out.

From the kitchen, one voice commented that there was no microwave. Odd, I thought, and went in to look. Sure enough. No microwave. People are strange when confronted with death. And people are funny when they poke around unfettered in someone else's space. We entertained ourselves with wave after wave of commentary about living without some damn microwave. The topic would die down and then float up again with new insights.

"Do you suppose she took out her frozen foods and cooked them in the oven?"

"I can't imagine!"

"Set in her ways!"

"Does she have a toaster?" Two of them began a shake-down of her kitchen cabinets. No toaster.

"Lord! She must have made her toast under the broiler in the oven!"

Then, since the mood had drifted from old Mrs. Shuler's death and her body just a few steps away, Darla, leaning against the door, almost as if she were afflicted by Tourettes, burst out with, "You know what you call an Amish man with his hand up a horse's ass?"

We froze mid-motion. Could she be telling a joke? Our behavior was disrespectful enough already.

"A mechanic!" she answered herself.

I snorted and the others suppressed a giggle. We looked away from each other in wonder at our separate reactions to death. Our straying off into humor. Whatever had we done to distort the graces of grief?

When the funeral people came (in my mind, two body

snatchers), I was delegated to go with them to check for any jewelry on her body. The three of us entered her bedroom and began breathing through our mouths - brown leakage showing through her panties. As the body snatchers untangled her from her sheet and checked her over, I grimaced at poor old Mrs. Shuler's face. Thinking how embarrassed she would be to know she wasn't tidy as a pin - and with three men looking at her body.

No jewelry at all.

As they moved her, I recalled finding my cat dead in the back yard when I was a boy. It was also stiff, though curled and solid as a Frisbee. I exited the room as the men began moving her onto the hand-held stretcher - two poles and canvas.

The rest of us watched, ranked like soldiers, as the snatchers carried Mrs. Shuler out into the hall and down the stairs. She seemed snug and cozy in the white, white sheets. They must have belted her stiff arms to her sides and strapped her to the stretcher to keep her from sliding off, I thought. To see her body shooting out over the stairs would have done me in.

The coroner announced that he was finished - that he and her attorney decided the Reverend Dr. Klemperer, her preacher, would be the one to call her niece in California.

I surrendered Mrs. Shuler's door key to the condo manager as she and I stood in the hall outside the door under the suspicious eyes of the others. The manager locked the door as the three of us, Darla, Janice, and I, watched. Each of us wary that she might return to continue searching for Mrs. Shuler's jewelry.

One by one, we left. The policeman, then the coroner. The EMS angel. And last, as a group, the manager, Janice, Darla, and I, walking down the quiet hallway girded by our involvement in the social heave of dealing with the death of a sweet old lady.

Amber, Wife and Mother

I am a fan of the writings of Virginia Woolf, her vast intelligence and post modern style of story telling with sentences that progress, zoom along and, often, seem never to end. This little short story could easily be written out with a more accessible style, but I wanted to stretch my writing wings. In addition, Virginia Woolf was a strong proponent for women's rights and intellects. Her interest in brilliant women and their interior lives ring true to me today. This story is fiction, though it may seem to be a story of every woman from an earlier generation, intimate and personal while looking into a mirror.

Amber, Wife and Mother

It is another morning in her home, Amber's home, and she is up before the others, a few quiet moments before the children "rise and shine" while her husband lingers in the bathroom; it is a slice of time available for herself and belonging solely to her, each of her senses fresh and alert, the quick cool air touching her body between the lifting off of her warm nightgown and the stepping into her cotton panties, her acrobatics with the bra - no hose or girdle this day - the feeling of cool slickness as her slip ripples down over her hips and thighs, and then the hoisting of the dress over her head, her favorite everyday dress with dark blue parallel lines aligned vertically, the dress with the open collar which her youngest likes on her, and, finally, now that all is ordered and agreeable to the process of dressing, the final events, the stepping into her sensible low-heeled shoes and taking a seat at her vanity, examining her face for a quick brush at the shock of brunette hair over to the right of her brow and checking her part on the left, and a touch, just a bare touch, of lipstick. Exactly at the contact of the pink lipstick to her lower lip, as if the act has signaled their approach, a deafening screaming and roaring of planes begin outside and overhead, the fighter planes, propeller driven, flying from McDill Field in Tampa where the airmen train for combat, for shooting and dogfights, a group of them, maybe six, to practice strafing the sand islands off shore, hitting targets, honing their skills at formation maneuvers. Later in the morning the big bombers will also thunder along the same path to practice dropping bombs at floating targets in the Gulf of Mexico. They come from the east of Amber's little town, and the Gulf is just a block away to the west, its great emptiness and silence reaching out toward the long sand islands paralleling the coast and convenient for perfecting practice runs and bombing. While Amber looks into the mirror, she counts in her mind the local war intrusions: fighters, bombers, amphibious tanks lumbering in the water, troop trains crowded with soldiers waving from the windows yet having no clear understanding of destination, military men seemingly everywhere in towns and cities, Red Cross drives, bond drives, blackouts at night, worship services, parades. She reaches for the powder puff and lightly touches it to her cheeks and forehead, but those motions are automatic and unstudied, ancillary to gazing into her hazel eyes, into those same eyes she studied as a child endeavoring, then, to understand her identity, her persona, her anima.

In that mirror-instance, that presentiment, Amber, wife and mother, visits herself, fully fleshed and visible, as a farm girl, pubescent, and she and her mother are walking to the farm of Amber's cousins, Hattie and Clara. It is that flavored stretch of time in the morning sun with quiet and rich earthy odors of farm life surrounding them, grasshoppers leaping and flying, brittle sounding and yellow. The cousins are like sisters to Amber - more than sisters - with whom she plays when the two families can be together - during special holidays, recess at the one room school, and while crops are being harvested. The three girls have bonded as only children who are isolated and introspective, hungry for companionship, can be - children building on the sweet intimacy that seems to belong only to them as they work together, explore and spy and compare each to each - the trio, Clara, Amber, and Hattie.

In the vanity mirror, Amber's right hand lifts to her left breast and touches it lightly; she is remembering how fascinating it was to her cousins and to her as their breasts slowly bloomed, the anxious, private times meant only for secrets. Those occasions, then, when Amber could spend the night with Clara and Hattie in the big feather bed across the hall from the boys' room, their doors closed, lights off, and the three cuddling together, their wordless explorations and easy bodies, the ecstasies of touching and the press of warm skin, this after the wide-eyed preparations for bed, standing naked at the washstand and sharing its two bowls of water, the sounds as first one and then the other used the honey bucket to pee in, the brushing of hair and soft whisperings and later, in bed, their warm hands and fingertips and quick kisses and the weights of warm flesh above, beside, and under, the feelings as though something inside Amber was squeezing her tailbone and buttocks. The silver moments when the private language of it all can only be silent.

Amber, wife and mother, remembers and smiles at the reflection smiling back at her - farm girl, wife, and mother.

Absolution

Again, I'm exploring the quiet moments of a woman while doing household chores. There is a time in the Mass when the priest holds up the golden paten, and I always think that he is somehow in the act of forgiving our sins like Jesus. Maybe I have scrambled dogma and dishwashing like a sloppy heretic.

What a glorious work
is a mother
in all ways
protector
nurturer
forgiver

Absolution

As she scrubbed
to loosen the carbonized food
from the bottom of the pan
she transformed herself into a priest
mindful of her son's sin
the charred red cardinal sin
of playing with matches

She thought
What about later
He is too young to bear the burden
of little Lauren's death

The decision came easy

When disputes of memory come due
let there be nothing lingering

She
the priest mother
wiped it dry
rinsed the pan solemnly
above the altar of her sink
expecting to encounter her own reflection
seeing instead her little boy
no longer condemned

Essy Barnett

An entirely fictional short story, a transcription by a young man of his great-grand father's ramblings telling about his early life and acquired sense of duty on the family farm. It is in two points of view. Turns out the old man, who had been a quiet store keeper, had a secret life.

Our best lessons
come to us
as children
it seems

Do we listen
to our elders
tell their secrets

Will we relate ours

Essy Barnett

The following is my transcription of the musings of my great-grandfather, Estes Barnett, as he sat on the porch of his home in Burleigh, Kentucky. He was ninety-four years old and died the next year. While he was relating this lovely story of his childhood, he rocked slowly in his porch chair and absently watched the traffic go and occasionally stopping to pat his old dog, Demon, who lay next to him and within easy reach. Pop, which is what we all called him, rambled on and on and probably would not have stopped if I had walked away. He was thin, a tall man with unusually good humor. However, he had attained that age in life when he remembered the distant past far better than the recent past. His eyes were clear, but his skin was mottled by age and hard work. Occasionally he would lean to one side and release some gas saying, "Must be some frogs here-abouts," and then chuckle to himself. I was certain it could easily wilt flowers.

And here is his recounting of an important time in his life. I am writing it mostly in modern English:

I had been out watching my favorite hen with her chicks when Mama called me in. "Your papa wants to tell you something," she said. She had been working dough for bread. I saw that her eyes were darting around the room and not settling on me. "Go on in to the front room. He's waiting for you."

Still barefoot, I walked into the room. There was a sick smell in there. The lantern's wick was set low, and Papa was on the good bed near the fireplace. Mama had a small fire going there. Lights from it were flickering. I walked up to the bed and stood above the trundle leaning my stomach against the frame of the big bed. Papa turned his head and looked at me, reached out and pulled me up closer to him, his arm around my back. There was a smell of rot coming from him. A sickening smell like a dead animal. Something bad coming out of my papa.

"Essy, you listen careful to what I have to say. You my boy. Ten year old now. Time you take on work like a man. Always remember to milk our cows like we been doing - at first light and just before sundown. Your momma depends on you to bring in the milk twiced a day. My sack so swole up and nasty, I don't think I can do it for a while. Old Doc Howard says I done ruptured myself lifting something too heavy."

I watched his face as he said the words. His forehead was slick with sweat and fever. The hairs on his face and chin were matted and coarse. I could feel his big hand on my back rubbing me as he did when he showed me he loved me. I said, "Yes, sir." I noticed the lights from the fireplace flickering across his face and eyes.

He patted my rump and said, "It's most time to go get the cows in. Better go on."

I looked at him, and he was looking at me. I stared into his eyes for a moment, and then he lifted his chin dismissing me. His eyes were on me when I turned toward the door. Mama was standing there. She had been watching us. Her hands were twisting her apron, and her face was closed, eyes open but firm and showing nothing.

I went past her and on out the kitchen door into the coolness of the late afternoon, into the field of new green grass. Our old farm dog, Bozo, came leaping and wagging up to go with me. He thought it was his duty to accompany me to get the cows in, but he just might stray off if he got wind of something more interesting. Bozo immediately began sniffing his way, staying ahead of me as I walked up the field toward the White Gate. We called it the White Gate even though it no longer had any white paint on it - hadn't since before I was born. Above us the sky was the barest blue.

As Bozo and I walked up the field, I thought about Papa's smell. Things that come out of things. Things that are rotten and stink. Things that are beautiful and good that sometimes produce badness. The apple trees rise up from the ground. Apples will come out of the blooms. Red and delicious. Pretty, good to smell, and wonderful to eat. Mama's pie and cider. But some will fall and rot and be ugly.

We went through the White Gate. I hooked it open for when we come back with the cows. The grass felt soft and cool to my toes and feet. Bozo stopped and looked at a clump of last summer's weeds near the fence post. He stood stock still staring. I walked over to see. There was the barest movement of a single blade of grass. A long snake, coal black, slowly and smoothly slid out in S curves paying no attention to either of us. We called this kind of snake a "cow sucker." A boy at school told me he saw one sucking on the tit of their cow. Papa laughed when I asked him about that and said never to bother cow suckers because they were our friends and eat mice and rats but never suck milk from a cow's tit. It curved its way silently down along the fence row. It moved with a different sureness than any other animal I knew.

When I turned and began walking out toward the cows, Bozo instantly forgot about the snake and romped ahead at full speed toward the middle of the field, up to the tobacco plant bed, a small plot of land where young and fragile tobacco seedlings were growing. It was surrounded by a split rail fence. Earlier our neighbors had come and helped clear and burn off the plant bed killing all the other seeds in the ground there. I looked at it and remembered the men working there, helping out because Papa was sick. The plant bed followed the contour of the ground. Our neighbors had covered it with burlap bags and feed sacks sewn together and stretched taut to protect the small plants underneath. The long cover was held above the young tobacco plants by wires that were stretched across every few feet. Bozo looked like he was about to run across the covering. I whistled and he stopped, looked back, and then changed his direction to where the cows were grazing.

This big field opened up to the sky. Papa told me that his own papa and grandpop had spent years clearing this field so that they could grow crops on it. I saw birds busy along its edges. From the time of the Indians, the earth had sent up trees and animals and maybe even the sky itself. My papa and his papa and his papa had cleared this big field so that it could give us tobacco and corn and wheat and hay. My bare feet touched the ground where they had worked so hard. The land and the sky, all of it was love and kindness to my eyes.

I saw our three cows with their heads lowered as they made their nibbles of grass. They were close together facing into the breeze, and quiet, barely a motion beyond a flip of the tail or ear. I called out to them. My call was like singing, beginning high and sinking down a-ways. I called them several times. Bozo was behind the cows and had decided to march them toward me. He began a different kind of barking at them. They each lifted their heads. I walked toward the cows saying "hay-ya, hay-ya" to them, and they began slowly plodding toward me with Bozo trotting along behind them. When we met, I started chanting "sook-sook-sook" as low as my voice could go while they clomped past me toward the White Gate. It gentled them somewhat. When Papa "sook-ed" them, they moseyed a little faster than for me. Their milk bags were full and sloshed from side to side as they walked. None of their tits was swollen. Papa told me always to check them for swollen tits. The same boy at school who told me about the snake sucking milk from his cow had also told me about how his papa had cured their cow of swollen tits. "In the light of the moon," he said, "Papa cut a long slit down the tail of their cow and put in sorghum molasses and pepper and then tied it up with a cloth." When I asked Papa about this, he bent over laughing.

After I took up my place behind our three cows, Bozo strayed off to explore his territory. Following the path through the White Gate, I heard it. The sound of the cow horn. It came from the house. The cow horn that hung by the back door. The pointed end had been cut off, and it could be sputtered into with tight lips in such a way that it made a sound like a music horn. It was the way neighbors could call to each other in an emergency. Mama was blowing the cow horn for the neighbors to hear. I looked for a fire. None. I looked and waited. The cows and Bozo stopped and faced the sounds. Mama blew it again and again. Long and fading sounds rising up and sliding back down ringing across the rolling land and disappearing. The sounds didn't belong to the green and blue and white of the land and sky and blooms. The sounds were ugly and came from my home. I knew it meant *come at once come at once help us help us!* It was Papa. Mama was calling about Papa. I could see Papa's eyes as he lay in the bed. I could smell the rot coming from him. Clinging to his lower lip was a dried crust of black vomit. And I remembered his words telling me how important it was to milk the cows.

The lead cow lifted her tail and dropped loose warm paddies. Ugly and smelly. We get good milk from her. Shit comes from her just like from us. Ugly and brown. Papa's sack and its rot coming out of him. Could it be that ugly and rotten things come from wonderful things? That inside all things there is hurt and pain that come out sometimes? The cow horn stopped. I closed the White Gate and hooked its chain over the nail. We continued our walk to the milk parlor in the barn. In my mind, I could hear Papa's words about duty.

We reached the barn. Before I opened the milk parlor door for the cows, I quickly poured some shelled corn and added an armful of hay into the trough at each stanchion, at each place where the cow stood to be milked. When I opened the milk parlor door, our cows rushed in, each to her usual place. I closed the wooden lock of the stanchion up to the neck of each cow to keep her from backing out while I was milking her. They began eating contentedly with an occasional switch of their tails.

Outside I heard the sounds of horse hooves and a buggy's wheels. Bozo was barking with excitement announcing the arrival of neighbors.

From their pegs on the wall, I lifted the little stool and the bucket that we always used. Papa had made them. I squatted down on the stool at the side of the first cow and began squeezing the milk out like I had learned from Papa. Taking white goodness from her. Although my hands were much smaller than his, I concentrated on the rhythm of squeezing - top finger-second finger-third finger-last over and over as I pulled down on her tit with an occasion bump upwards into her bag to remind her to let down her milk. Papa could make the milk foam when it sprayed into the bucket. I got the milk out slowly but surely. I used the papa bucket first and half filled it. Then got down the grand-pop bucket for the last cow.

Bit by bit, one thing after the other, I finished the milking and turned the cows out. It was becoming dark, and the beauty of the spring day was disappearing into blackness. As I struggled carrying both buckets heavy with the milk from our three cows, I looked at the house and saw lights moving inside. Down the lane I heard people talking, and another horse coming toward us. Someone was at the well drawing up water. Good water from deep in the earth.

I had finished milking like Papa told me.

Pop got up and went into the house after he reached this point in his story. I had taped all of it to transcribe later. My plan was to give it as gifts to my cousins and other family members whenever he should die. It would make a great memorial, I thought. Especially knowing, as we do now, that he had been a hired executioner for wardens and sheriffs in seven states when he was a younger man. That was back before capital punishment was outlawed.

He owned a small town dry-goods store here then - "Essy's DryGoods and General Merchandise." We found out later that as an executioner he went by the name Estes Taylor Cross instead of the name we know him by, Essy Barnett. He had it worked out with those wardens and sheriffs who needed his services to telegraph him in a coded message so that no one around these parts would know he was an executioner. Pop would announce that he had to go on a business trip for his store, and he would return a week later with good money in his pocket. Since he was a highly respected man in town, no one ever suspected that he might have gone off for reasons other than to tend to his business.

Many years later, when his grown children found out that he had been the executioner of so many men and a few women, they agreed to keep it a secret. But you know what tight little towns are like. The secret lasted about three days. Instantly the town was aghast at this news. Everyone talked about it, and the story made the local newspaper and the big Louisville papers. He was an instant celebrity. Of course it didn't hurt his business. Soon after he sold out, retired, and was armed and ready to entertain any listeners with his tales of days long gone.

Reporters came and asked him all sorts of questions: "Did you feel apprehension or remorse in pulling the lever to hang someone?"

"Not at all. In fact, I treated each criminal with respect, and before I placed the hood over their heads each one usually, in one way or another, said they forgave me because they knew I was just doing my job. Each time I made sure that the knot and the trap worked and that they died quickly. Not one of my criminals went to glory after a struggle or needing a second hanging."

"Did it bother you to do this, Mr. Barnett, er, Mr. Cross?"

"No. I have a fine sense of duty that I learned as a child."

First Kiss

Well, yes, this one is a partly fictional account of my own tender first kiss in college which will seem unimaginably restrained to some readers. It is a simple, first person, linear story.

Do you remember
your first kiss
was it with sweaty hands
and bursting heart
that set you free

First Kiss

It was an innocent time in Conner's life, his freshman year in college just five years ago, safely a thousand miles away from his family and home. Free and independent at last. Looking at all the new faces and unfamiliar places, thinking to himself, *Does a person ever actually belong to a place?* Anyone looking at Conner would notice, without question, his tenseness, the bundling of strength ready to leap out of him perhaps like a stone resting in a tight slingshot. Armed, cocked, and ready to fly into new experiences.

He was not unlike so many other freshmen there in college, excited to explore other people and places and ideas, not to mention actions up to now forbidden for even the least consideration. Anxious to be an active member among new faces with unfamiliar privileges approvable or not by the censors back home. And also, no more dreaded home-schooling and its rank solitude, its exclusivity and narrowness.

And, mark this, Conner's dental braces had been removed at long last, the kind with rubber bands to pull back his bucked teeth. Four years of tonguing the metal hardware. Yes, they termed the wires "hardware." Every few months the orthodontist wrenched at a wire and tightened the tug on his beavers. And now the whole kit-and-caboodle was gone. Throughout his days, he would catch himself sliding his tongue along the outside of his upper teeth, feeling the smooth contours, the orderliness of his teeth. It had become the supreme gift to him, the ticket for belonging to a peer group without having to cover his mouth when he spoke or laughed or talked. Freedom to grin and speak unencumbered as an equal among the others, the real people, the handsome and beautiful. Maybe he could gain open acceptance from others and a permanent riddance of feelings of shame and worthlessness. No one here would know of that lost deformity and the scarceness of possibilities. Wearing his retainer at night would bear little importance, easily slipped out and tucked into his pajama pocket around others.

Along with these geographic and physical blessings, he was far from his family's church. One of those very conservative, wealthy, protestant ones which will remain unnamed at this time (But it begins with *Pr...*). A fine building with row on row of proper, pewter-haired ladies with perfect teeth accompanied by their fusty, well-mannered menfolk.

On looking around his campus those first few days and nights, the others seemed far less threatening and complicated than he had expected. More fun-loving and casual. How many times had Conner heard, "Be grateful you are home-schooled and don't have to be with those wild public school boys and girls...?" That along with the ready indictments of church members, especially from those pewter-haired women which plagued him worse. Their up-right admonitions: "Nothing in excess. No indulging in loud joy and laughter. And absolutely no approaches to sex or its related expressions." With relief, Conner realized he had survived. Their supreme message echoed more and more faintly: "Avoid any indulgences beyond the barest or suffer the disapproval of God." It was becoming clear to him that he had escaped that life before it was too late, escaped battered and struggling among waves of personal shame and guilt, those puritanical dogmas which his church and parents had hammered into him.

How those people managed to reproduce was a continuing mystery to him. Surely they didn't *do it*. You know... ! IT! Conner's instructions about sex were limited to his biology text and secret self-explorations - you know, frequent, top-secret mastur...! "Sorry. Out of our sense of dignity, let's skip that salacious word - the very idea of it is offensive," as they would say.

Even though he was ordinary in body and mind, Conner had been sheltered by his family, and, to be honest, also by himself - out of obedience, he supposed. But, he harbored a staggering number of questions about his own sex and the opposite sex.

Girls his age remained a continuing mystery. In his college classes, they were obviously smarter and much quicker to brown-nose the professors than the boys were. Or should they be termed "young men" and "young women" instead of "boys" and "girls?"

He noticed the upper-class students, so much more adult with their suave, relaxed faces, were set apart from his freshmen level. They paid little attention to the younger ones with their monkey faces, obviously freshly minted college students and somewhat brainless by comparison. Still decked out in the latest fads. Wide-eyed, self-conscious, and tripping over their own feet.

He openly gawked at how so many of the young women displayed their boobs. Can we dub them that? "Tits" would be too impolite, surely. The exposed vee between them calling for attention. So many beautiful *racks.* That's what he heard his roommate say. "Racks." After Conner's classes and observing all those "racks" and "vees," he'd just have to head to a quiet bathroom booth in the Student Union. And later, each time, he'd be weak-kneed with those pestering flames of shame and guilt.

In the dorm the first night, Conner listened intently to a country boy, more experienced (and, he suspected, possibly not a virgin) tell about trying to unsnap a bra during steamy struggles in the back of his car. "By god, each time I tried to get that dang thing alose, Earlene would swell up just like my horse whenever I tried to tighten the cinch to go riding." Obviously not home-schooled. As the other boy related this, Conner's mouth became juiced up, and he thought of how he looked to the others - so much immature boy beaming from his face. The other guy was everything Conner wanted to be. A young man who could act the way he felt and felt the way he acted.

Looking around, Conner realized each guy in the dorm room brimmed with unspoken stories of kissing and sexual successes and failures. There he sat on his roommate's bed with two others hoping that his purity and innocence did not beam out like a searchlight from his face. The truth was, Conner had never worked up enough nerve to kiss a girl outside of his mother, sister, and, some years before, two aunts towering above him who grabbed him up and insisted on lip kisses - their lips compressed into a deadly tight line below their bleached mustaches.

At Tampa International, just as Conner turned to walk away from his family seeing him off, his mother popped him a little stinger on the side of his neck. That caused the right side of his body to tingle and go partially numb. It stayed that way all the way to the huge airport in Atlanta. Just a simple kiss, even if it came from his mother. He thought, *Will I ever be able to kiss a real girl? You know. Kiss like movie stars.*

How many times, though, alone in bed at night, had he worked over his pillow, wagging his head like a man kissing Doris Day (so what if he liked those old black and white movies - he wasn't allowed to see a PG or R rated ones) while secretly fondling the corner of his pillow and trying mentally to turn it into a breast ("titty," whatever), soft and willing. Ah, the dreams of what his first kiss would be! Soft and natural. Surely followed by unchained passion and little nips and sweetness and moaning from her as she would pull him into a tighter embrace and he would wrap his arms around her - captivated by the sudden awareness of warmth from her full chest.

When the time came, surely Conner would know instinctively what to do. Where his hands would go. How to tilt his head so their noses wouldn't crash into each other. And, above all, how to keep from cracking his front teeth against hers. Or, horrors, suddenly sneezing on her. Would she slip him her tongue? Oh, yuk! He hoped not.

To make a long story short, after two anxious weeks, Conner finally worked up a date. He was all set to lose this unblemished bud of his youth, so to speak - to kiss a girl not kin to him. To plant one on her like a real man.

Fast forward past all the pre-date jibberish to the conclusion of that night, THE NIGHT OF CONNER'S FIRST KISS. It was fifteen minutes before she needed to be in her dorm room. Now that his braces were gone and he had remembered to remove his retainer earlier as he splashed Brut Aftershave Lotion on his freshly shaved cheeks, Conner had completed the requisite preparations that the other boys did before they rushed out to their romantic conquests - the ones they had been bragging to him about.

She and Conner had seen a movie and had walked back to campus. They sat on a tier high up in the outdoor stadium. A place near the girls' dorm where young lovers went, he'd heard, to smooch. Here they were, a petit, sophisticated city girl, and Conner, a goofy, innocent, small town boy. She was quick-witted with bright red lipstick that, Conner thought, colored and heated the scene around them. And she had arched black eyebrows that reminded him of racing stripes on a hot car. But best of all, cuddled in her thin blouse were those pointy knockers and the vee between them - which he memorized to describe later that night in the dorm.

It was a quiet, cool night with romance buzzing around them, it seemed to him. They sat. Spoke little inanities back and forth. And sat some more. Twitchy, on Conner's part. His brain bursting with activity fully aware of the depths of the flesh - and an iguana or some other small animal moving around in his pants. She was patient but with a look on her face of watching for something to happen, and possibly she was amused at his struggling, his tactics, his greedy, sweaty hand in hers. That hand-holding bit took a major amount of brave manipulation on Conner's part. Only one other time had he worked up to that victory - last year back home in a Doris Day movie under the cover of darkness and away from the eyes of public school boys sitting farther back - out of pop-corn throwing range.

But tonight, he prayed this girl wouldn't pick up on the tumult crashing around in him as he labored, as he edged his way toward this momentous kiss. Somehow, Conner figured, since this was the place where others casually smooched, it would be easy for him. By osmosis, maybe.

With the reckless abandon of a lover, did he really begin each sentence with the word "Baby?" Probably something he considered manly that he'd heard uttered to ole Doris while she flapped her eyelids waiting for the hot kissing to begin. Did he actually say, with a voice like an oboe, "Baby, have you finished reading *The Return of the Native* yet?" Or, even worse, "Baby, I think you are so sophisticated." Topped by, "Baby, do you like to kiss?" How suave and debonair he felt. However, that last one made him realize he needed to pee. Each time he stumbled through a "Baby..." sentence, she giggled, and it sounded full-throated and mature and sophisticated far beyond Conner's humble attainments in the realm of romance.

By now, in the spaces of furious silence, his hearing had become muted over by the sounds of blood rushing in his head. Finally, finally - probably exhausted by his adolescent foreplay - this goddess took the lead, simply leaning toward Conner and tilting her head. He gasped audibly in realization that The Time Had Come. So, no longer deadened by timidity, he closed his eyes and inched forward. No sparks. No tongue. No braces. No clutching embrace of his chest against those beautiful boobs. Just a sweet, simple kiss that lasted maybe through the count of two. His face lit up burning with heat.

And, sagging a bit in relaxed comfort, Conner pulled back from her, adjusted his sitting position, and - hold on, folks - he farted. A quick, sharp, very loud popper that, indeed, did not smell like sweet basil.

What else could poor old Conner do? He shoved her away - and fled, his arms flapping like a sidewalk lunatic and the cool night air brushing past his face.

There was no mistaking. For further humiliation, Conner heard her laughing loudly behind him, her musical voice bouncing across the football field and in counterpoint to the sound of his shoes pounding out a beat back to the dorm - to the lies he would tell there. And to the lies he would hear there.

Conner had finally kissed a girl.

Identity

A poem about the struggles one endures attempting to zero in on self, that unending quest. I've read some of the Roman writings about making decisions by observing a bird in the air. If it flies to the left, a bad omen, and, if to the right, a good sign to resolve a question.

Left side
the unlucky side
or to the right
the side of good fortune
Romans thought

Where will I find my self
at age five
thirteen
twenty-five
or seventy

I wonder

Identity

Who am I
I know
and don't know
but it consumes me
and has since I was a child
in that place
they called home

On the one hand
I am aloft
standing in a tree
high
hidden in yellow leaves
lightly brushing my skin
with shadows and light

On the other
I am on a beach
the sole witness
of water's infinity
of water's eternity
my hands reaching out to them
my feet no longer shuffling
in the loose sand

And now
immobile
I look left
to my past
and right
to my now
and what will be

This is both harsh
and hopeful

Sensitivity

One thing I have learned about the human brain is that we know very little about how it works and what it can do. I assert that children and old folks are unimaginably able to permit their brains to soar far beyond the ordinary. This story has bits of surrealism and is basically linear with a somewhat single point of view.

Who knows
the power of a brain
free in the breeze
while loafing
at the waterfront
alongside
another old coot

Sensitivity

I was there at the waterfront marina which retained scant semblance to the same place fifty years earlier. In front of me, expensive boats, yachts, and sailboats, all of them docked and rather superfluous, it seemed to me - somewhat like me as I strolled around looking, this time as an old man. Yep. Old fart. Unlike some old geezers I know, my knowledge base had not in the least reached unbearable extremes even though I was no longer burdened by the baggage of my first years here, in this west coast Florida town now subsumed by the megalopolis of Tampa and St. Pete, its urban sprawl heaving behind me as I looked out over the water to the dark line of sand islands farther off shore. I stood facing into the clear breeze with the old town behind me, a pretty place all colorfully landscaped with mini-parks and red brick streets twisting around neat gardens and comfy little shops and walking paths - a tourist destination populated by well dressed affluent people looking, looking, looking at all the eye candy that decorated Dunedin. I had come here for a visit, taking a break and standing at the waterfront watching the ospreys, the pelicans, and gulls. Even a spoonbill roseate bird trolling in the shallows for tiny living things.

Can a man like me, who grew up here, look at this scene and not animate each of his senses? Can a human, any man or woman or child facing an ocean (or the Gulf) fail to see the music of the air or taste the motions of the water's rumpled surfaces or hear the colors there? I give credit that I am not alone in this, for most people also have sharp sensitivities, I suspect.

On occasions I might look over at another person and speak gently, at which they respond kindly and with equally perceptive ownership of their words as we unite in a simple bond of friendliness. Never fails. Maybe that is because I am now elderly and have that simple look of trust and innocence which sweetens late life. At last, no longer a poisonous young man. Or maybe it is because one look at me and the other person knows we are, at least for these few moments, sharing the same life. I love that part of living. Listening. Empathizing. Soft words afloat in the air between us.

But there is more. Somewhere way back, perhaps as a child listening to old folks rocking and sipping their ice water on shaded screened-in porches under great live oaks, I realized that if I pulled closely, I could make out what they weren't putting into words. Could catch a sound here and there beneath their active speech. Pick out from their tones and body gestures the unspoken and draw out the molecular structures of non-verbal thoughts swirling around in their mental undercurrents. Perhaps all people have this ability and practice it for amusement. Or at least they did when they were children.

So, I turned from facing the bay and walked to a nearby bench in the shade where another old codger was sitting. Room for at least two more, and I sat without asking and without apology, no doubt interrupting his reverie. His eyes fixed at something a thousand yards away. Or maybe just three inches in front of him. Ancient eyes. He barely glanced sideways at me, and he scooted slightly to his left to make room or to widen the space between us. We sat quietly. I wondered if maybe he would speak to me with an oboe voice. Should I clear my throat, moisten my reeds, or tune my strings warning him that I have something to say? But he and I remained silent. A slight forward and back motion by both of us, the solace of solitude being our afternoon snack. From the quick look I had of him, I recognized that he was the sort who easily seems to know what there is that doesn't immediately meet the eye and who understands what is on the other side of things - a man like me who has an honorable pact with solitude in his old age.

The salted breeze parted over our faces and whispered in our ears. Our lungs clear and taking in the air coming from the Gulf of Mexico across the islands and over St. Joseph's Sound to us. For a moment, we both watched an osprey floating, circling above the fish house. The two of us united in awe at its flight.

It was easy. I pulled with my mind and entered his, into his swift moving tableaux of non-verbal images, some in color and many in black and white or negatives of them. He was scanning rapidly. I saw myself there also, a flicker among platoons of people. Hordes of men and women flashing through his memories. Lines and rooms-full. People in varieties of clothing and styles. Some who were still children. Laughing women. Crying children. And hairy men. People. Red-headed, praying, singing, naked, fighting, learning, running, searching, working people. Yes. Working. This chumpy old man next to me had been, above all else, a working man. Picking up a cascade of work-place images, I realized that I had zeroed in on him, learning about him and his loyalty to work, to his vocation.

Recognizing what I was doing made me keenly aware and a little embarrassed of my intrusion into his musings. My mind game. I blinked and let my attention run forward, out to a pelican perched on the top of a piling. The old bird extended its wings partly and lifted its beak. Then it settled into its waterfront pose for the tourists and for us. More silence from the old man next to me. Not a furious silence. Was he watching the pelican, too? A mutual attention to distract our idle musings?

I returned to my mental amusement, a departure from within myself. My bench companion was reliving, in careful detail, a time close to here, on a shaded road named Victoria Drive, barely long enough to front four or five houses. He is there, standing on the shale surface of the road. A summer boy. Maybe fifteen years old. Intense. Soaking in the close night-time isolation favored by tormented adolescents. Walking and examining, taking inventory of this favored nocturnal place in front of the series of old Victorian gingerbread houses. White houses just a few yards back from the grassy shoreline where fiddler crabs, busy knitting their legs, clicking, were swarming over the moon white sand. Back from the road, the houses were glowing in nighttime gray. And he stopped and studied a narrow wooden pier stretching out into the bay directly in front of the middle house. It stood with a roofed-over structure at its end. He examined the exclusivity of it and whistled a few notes out to its gazebo.

The five large gingerbread houses behind him interrupted and drew at him, conversing with the boy there on Victoria Drive, a name that fits the houses because the flavor of that era had swept in and around and over and under them while they were being built. Add to that the great mossy oaks and pines and the tall hedges of poinsettias around the porch of the middle house. Azaleas with their white flowers, eyes in the night, fronting the others. Everything as it should be. The sight of them comforting the young man. Their continuance and beauty offering him a strong sense of permanence and dependability to offset his unsettling transience.

The old man next to me continued seeing himself there in the shape of the boy looking at the yellow orange lights from the windows. A long brightness reaching out to him through a screened door. Voices from a radio inside. A woman and man talking. A distant cough. He, the boy, invisible and worthless and alien. Just a no-count Florida Cracker Boy treading in the depths of other people and inaccessible places. Maybe he was hearing the skirl and keening of bagpipes playing in his Scottish DNA.

Then it occurred to me. Could my bench companion also be dipping into the well of my own thoughts? What was he picking up layered beneath my surface pictures, my silent flow of wordless images? Maybe that time when I let my hands go and played the Prokofiev sonata - released them because I could not consciously force control onto them. The amazement that blew out of my head as one hand played different music than the other at the same time. And all the while I was not watching them. Only listening and soaring, soaring, climbing above me into another dimension at last, at last into freedom, freedom, free of dominion. Could he be visualizing and paralleling along with me?

Maybe we were merely two surly old coots sitting on opposite ends of a bench mentally catching cats by their tails, wolves by their ears, and sharks by their fins. Both of us traveling into our individual existential meltdowns? So much boy remaining in each of us. The two of us caught up in slipstreams behind those poorly remembered rapid years. Tripping over moments needing reappraisal amid the twanging sounds of cables hitting the masts of sailboats moored in the marina before us.

I promise you, honor bright, during those few minutes on the bench, I became a part of that other man as I delved into his memories. He and I. Both standard issue, though fusty now. Not resembling either real men or poultry. Neither of us plot bound. Just two old stumps keenly aware that the passage from *will be* to *is* to *was* has become shorter and shorter.

Did both of us silently gaze at that posturing pelican and find ourselves with a weak present and fading pasts as we searched about for our futures? Am I hamstrung, now, to the sweet chaos of my sensitivities?

Summation

In this poem I am remembering anxiously awaiting the arrival of my oldest brother, Bobby, returning home on leave after being in Korea and healing from his wounds.

What is it like
for a soldier
on returning home
after years away

What words
can he say
to it all

Summation

We met him at the train
the toom toom sounds from the engine
and I caught first sight of him
my oldest brother
as he stepped onto that metal stool
the conductor placed
onto the ground
of our hometown

He had been ten years away
in uniform and a war

I watched his eyes
to see if he knew us
if he remembered me

His smiles were quick
with some disdain and edgy fright
as we walked the short distance
into our yard
and all he said was
"The trees have grown."

The Faux War

I was a child during World War II. That was a time, still, when children often formed small groups to roam the streets and neighborhoods, and, since we lived close to the waterfront of our little town, usually we stopped by there once a day. The interior tales in this short story were told to me during those halcyon days. The false war we imagined was real and a part of our lives.

A time it was
during that war
even in the sunshine state

While the big folks
conserved and sacrificed
and soldiers and sailors
trained and fought,
boys and girls
endured their own struggles
their imagined wars

The Faux War

It was during the time of the Marine Detachment which increased the population of Dunedin, Florida, by three hundred to approximately 1,800 people during WWII. To every citizen, at that time, the war was clearly between "us and them," "them" being the Japanese and the Germans. The black-and-white newsreels showed the realities of war: cities in ruins, displaced people, bodies and more bodies, soldiers goose-stepping, ships burning, bombers and fighter planes and search-lights, dirty children with stricken eyes. Local women met in churches to roll bandages, and they took classes in first aid. To all, the war was real, but it was out there, far away. At night, volunteers, two at a time, climbed the steps and ladder to the top of the wooden observation tower, actually a four-story addition to the wooden library building at the water front, to watch for lights out on the Gulf of Mexico, possible signals from U-Boats. There were blackouts when all the lights along the coast had to be extinguished - an eerie time of total darkness. A deep time when children shivered inside their homes, within the black darkness, hearing adults whispering - children visualizing invasions and the real war blasting and howling at the very edges of Dunedin. And don't forget rationing - tokens and coupon booklets required for purchasing meat, sugar, shoes, gasoline and other essentials.

The Marine Detachment was housed in green tarpaper wooden buildings at the old airfield up at the northern end of town on the edge of the bay. The Marines were brought in to learn how to use the newly invented amphibious tanks - called Ducks. These war machines evolved from rudimentary swamp buggies into small landing crafts to haul maybe fifteen to twenty infantrymen each from the mother ship to whatever beachhead was being assaulted. No doubt, you have seen those pictures of landings on the Pacific islands during WWII and dead Marines bloated on the shore. But that was later. These were training/experimental machines, and they were being modified from month to month in the rush to that time when small, open, tank-tread, armored vehicles would be necessary to deposit soldiers on beaches quickly, the men huddled in them with no overhead protection. After they bobbed up onto the beaches, a ramp dropped at the front, and the men poured out.

The Marines practiced and trained out in the bay between the mainland and the sand islands off shore, about a mile due west. Noisy, cumbersome, foam makers. The track on each side of the amphibious tank looked like a Sherman tank's track only they were all metal with what the local boys and girls called "scoops" that could dig into the beach sand and also provide propulsion in water. To watch them churning in the bay, practicing and training, was awesome for children. And the war planes. Huge bombers thundering low over Dunedin and out to the Gulf of Mexico on training missions. The fighter planes, much smaller, practiced strafing parts of the islands and resembled distant birds diving, the sounds reaching the mainland after the fighters were soaring up into the sky again, turning for another run. An unforgettable collection of war sounds.

To summer boys and girls, all of this was a safe war, a faux war: amphibious tanks, bombers with men waving down from the bubbles underneath, fighters ripping past and dipping their wings at the waving children, and the troop trains going north, filled with soldiers - also waving. Maybe waving goodbye.

Although all of this seemed harmless and far removed from what children watched in the newsreels and saw in each Life Magazine, there remained a suspicion that the real war was also edging about in the shadows of their lives. Threats, hazards, horrors, and monsters lurking all around out in the bay, in the swamps further east, and even at night in their neighborhoods. Children needed to be careful and to stay close to each other - and not stray too far from their homes and mothers. Especially, they had to watch and listen to what others were talking about - to tell each other any news about war-like threats and dangers that might come to them. After all, in their minds, any danger to their lives in Dunedin was equal to the great war that was going on in other places.

What the various small gangs of children and teenagers passed along among themselves was personal and secret - not for adults to know anything about. Any talk about dangers took on the face of war and was mercurial and short lived from day to day - perhaps hour to hour. Sometimes news traveled from the younger to the older, but most often from the older down to the naïve and altruistic little folks, usually younger brothers and sisters - those who kept a close eye and hungry ear to what the big ones were up to.

The report on one particular summer day was about a sixth grade girl, "She fell off the end of the pier and a shark was coming at her and she was splashing and yelling but a giant squid came to her rescue and grabbed the shark with all of its arms and saved the girl until she could dog paddle to the little beach by the marina." Such an epic fight, between the squid and the shark! Like two soldiers in hand-to-hand combat in the war. The bigger boys who witnessed it vowed that the shark actually howled and grunted, and the squid wrapped the shark up so tightly that she (the emphasis was that the squid, the savior, was a "lady squid") drowned the evil shark, the thrashing of its tail slowly weakening until it stopped moving. This enemy was now dead, defeated by the good lady squid. Maybe the Marines trained it. The young girl was saved and safe.

When word reached Gary and his small tribe of about-to-be fourth graders, the five of them rushed to the marina hoping to see the body of the shark, the lurking enemy. There it was on its side, at the water's edge in the weeds under the blazing sun. Its underside white, smooth, and swollen - its back coal black with white tiger stripes on its flank. Its mouth gaped open, and rows of pointed teeth gleaming. The dead enemy. As they approached, carefully, tentatively, the gulls flew away squalling at them. The group circled around the shark and looked for its eye - the one that should be visible on the side of the carcass. Gulls had already pecked at the open gashes on its great body. They must have gotten to the eye first.

The five of them, shoulder to shoulder, stared. Patsy leaped back screaming and ran. "I seen it move its mouth! I did! I did! He's gonna jump and eat us up!" There was unanimous and instant belief as they fled to safety further inland. Their feet bare and tender. They ran awkwardly ever on the look-out for prickly-pears and sandspurs. Each one certain that if the shark could not actually die, then no enemy could remain defeated. After all, the Japanese and the Germans didn't seem to back off from war and the loss of their own soldiers.

In moments, the children were huddled behind the azaleas around the side porch of the old library building next to the shuffleboard courts. The talkative ones, Judy and Donnie, commenced to chatter about all of this news - the sixth grade girl, the battle of the shark and squid, and the dead shark that wasn't quite dead.

Frankie brought out from under the flooring of the library porch, from his secret hiding place there, a cigarette - rather half of one. And a kitchen match. Both items eliciting eye-darts of unmistakable devilment from each child. Patsy and Gary and Judy and Donnie became silent. Watching.

Frankie had white hair. The smoke from the match was white also. He held the match until it quit making little sparks, then put the end of the cigarette to the flame enough to make a glow. He handed the burning match to Judy who watched the flame work its way down toward her finger tips before she stuck it in the gray sand, and he put the cigarette stub between his lips and took in a puff. White smoke was rising from the end of the cigarette, and Frankie let the smoke fall out of his mouth. The four watched this procedure in wonder, and Gary said he could already feel the back of his mother's hairbrush on his bottom if she smelled the cigarette smoke on him.

It was quiet Donnie with the crooked eyes, though, who said, "I heard about a big snake." Florida children universally had nightmares about snakes, the result of their parents' frequent admonitions about rattlers and moccasins and coral snakes. In their minds, all snakes were poisonous and would aggressively slither through the grass to bite boys and girls. Mothers warned, "Never pick up a ribbon in the grass." Tarzan movies showed boa constrictors that, no doubt, lurked in the neighborhood bamboos and brush and palmettos of the empty lots around Dunedin. They carried with them a danger equal to war.

Donnie spoke up, "My big brother told me about a place near Lake Okeechobee where a giant snake lived for a bunch of years and it grew and grew until you could see its eyes in the night and the eyes were far apart."

This bit of news gained their instant attention.

"How far apart?"

Donnie held his arms out from his shoulders and wiggled his finger tips. "This far."

The other four sat side by side - close, as young ones in a circle do.

"One time a rancher saw it swaller a whole cow, horns and all."

Brief pause of wonder.

"The Seminole Indians said it had lived near the big lake for hundreds of years and would eat just about anything." He stopped to pick at a scab on his knee. "My big brother said there was a fire that burned under the ground. He said it burned slowly under the grass and dirt. And if a person didn't know where the fires was burning, he could drop down into the fire and burn up."

By then Frankie had spit on the end of the cigarette and replaced it under the floor of the library's porch.

"I asked Simon how ground could burn, and he told me it was not really ground but something called peat. And that old snake was slithering along over the peat fire and the ground caved in and he was burned up. 'Just like Hell,' he told me. Later on the ranchers found its bones. They were all that was left of that giant snake. And a fully grown man stepped inside the ribs and walked around without stooping over."

At that, there was full approval of this story followed by general scratching of itchy places. Gary had started it by digging at his head.

It was that same Gary who said, "The Cat Man was at our neighbor's back windows last night. The screaming and yelling woke me up."

Now each of this band of naïfs knew with certainty about the Cat Man - another enemy of good people - its green eyes and its sharp claws that scratch at the screen windows of pretty older sisters. Men, hearing the screams, would come with their guns to chase it away, but they never could catch him even though they were like the good soldiers in war.

Gary continued, "Momma told me it was true. He would scratch and bite little boys, too. So, when the street lights go on, I had better be inside the house."

It was Frankie's squeaky voice that caught their attention, none of them wanting to leave. "I know how I got my white hair." The tone of his voice and the look on his face indicating they wouldn't believe him. The others looked at him, tilting their heads a bit, looking and waiting. He continued, "When I was little I stuck my tongue on both of those things at the top of a dry cell battery and got a shock.

My brother told me my hair stood up and I had sparks shootin'
off my fingernails. And the next morning my hair was white."

The reply from the others was in unison.

"Naw!"

"Didn't neither!"

"... fibbin'!"

After a pause, Gary, still thinking about snakes, added,
"My big brother got sick from kissing his girlfriend after she
got bit by a rattlesnake. And he got all swoled up."

Judy asked, "How come she didn't die if she got bit by a
rattler?"

"They took her to the hospital and she got well. But
now her spit is poison."

This bit of information caused eyes to enlarge.

Donnie spoke next, with certainty and total belief, "I
saw a snake, uh, one time, uh, and it was rolling down the
sidewalk hanging onto its tail. Like a hoop. And it chased me
all the way into my yard and up on the porch."

At this, the others leaned a bit forward and opened
their mouths in awe. From off in the distance they heard a
woman's soprano voice calling, "Patsy! Patsy Ann! Time to
come home!"

At this, the five gentle children, satisfied, emerged
from the azaleas and turned toward their homes out of harm's
way from any dangers of war, real or imaginary.

Interlude on the Bay

Maybe the father in this story is taking this son along to fish with him as an effort to become closer in a relationship that lacks intimacy. It is a post-modern, non-linear short story in three points of view.

There are raw times
in the contests
between fathers and sons
even while fishing
from a boat
with full white sails

Interlude on the Bay

A father and son gone fishing together. The morning sky is an aluminum glow. The two on a single-mast boat out in the bay between the islands and the shoreline, the mainsail full and bulging. Sitting at the stern managing the rudder is the father, and the boy stands at the bow with one hand gripping the mast for balance. Clean, clear air in the mainsail pulls the boat smoothly across the calm water, and musical gurgling sounds follow them from the wake behind the rudder. The tide is coming in swiftly and silently from the Gulf of Mexico, into the channel between the two long sand islands.

"It'll be good fishing in the channel," the man announces, more like a bark toward his youngest son who looks back at him, at his father wearing a ragged old fedora and white shirt. He takes careful notice of his father's lips, their default position in a frown as if there is a pebble in his shoe. The man is rough-edged and has survived the harsh histories of the Great Depression and both world wars. A Southern gentleman to his wife and to strangers. However, not so to his children. Especially to this son. Even the father's body language speaks out, *I am the father. Must be respected and obeyed. Always. Life is unfair. The world deserves my rancor.* His own youthful innocence had turned into an extended, stinging loss considering what he had possessed and what his children take for granted. The act of paternity became a painful disability for him as he observed his offspring stalking through adolescence. This son in particular. His youth irritates his father. The boy's rapid growth into manhood threatens him also. And the boy's pals are disrespectful and give the father snide looks from time to time.

A father and son in ritual conflict - out fishing together.

That one there, the fifth one. Staring at the channel marker as if Jesus were nailed to it. Not rambunctious like his brothers. Shy. Scared of me. Good. Keep him afraid of me.

"Just stay out of my way and do what you're told. Raise the jib when I tell you."

Looks like we'll be at my favorite spot by the time the sun's fully up. Fine day. Low breeze. Mainsail's full and tight. We're moving quietly. At last, no noise. No trains. No tourists asking blame-fool questions. Other men jealous to have my depot job. Feed and clothe the family, and my children only come to me if they need spending money. My parents never gave me money for movies - or paid to straighten my teeth. I get no thanks from my sons and daughter. Ever.

"Toss that anchor over onto the mud flat. We'll cast our lines in the channel and catch us a few trout. Good eating."

Great Scott! That boy almost threw himself in with the anchor. Can't he do anything right? I'll have to do all the catching, seems.

"Oop-oop! First strike!"

Silver flash. About ten inches. Solid body. Good filets.

"Hoo! Looks like you've got one, too. Don't jerk it. Pull it in slowly. Don't you know how to catch a fish?"

Always stupid. Sissy boy.

Mother said it won't be bad if I do what he tells me and stay out of his way. But I've never fished from a sailboat before. What if....? Jib?

"What's a jib, sir?"

Daddy's looking at this smaller sail up front. And that rope.

"Yes! Pull that sheet rope till the little sail is all the way up! Now tie it!"

Later the father turns the boat into the wind and unties

the sheet rope to the mainsail, letting it down. With his eyes, he instructs the boy to lower the jib. Then he nods at the anchor and jerks his head toward the water.

"The anchor? Yes, sir."

Heave ho, the anchor! Oops! Almost tripped over my own feet. We're out in the bay pretty far. Would he let me drown? Probably get so mad he'd leave me for the sharks. Can't stand the sight of me. Never a smile. Glares at me. Big bully. Somebody said I have his eyes. I don't want to look like him in any way.

Quiet. Yeah. Just the sounds of gulls and the breeze. And his little hacking coughs and grunts. Maybe he likes this. That awful tune he whistles through his teeth. The very way he breathes drives me....unh! A tug! Must be a strike! Reel it! Will he reach out and grab the line? He's not really looking at me, just the line in the water. Bet he'll be angry I caught one, too. I didn't do it on purpose. What am I supposed to do with it?

I couldn't have come from his nuts. Ew! Don't even think about it. Does he suspect my secrets?

Trappers on Return

Two men
bonded by love of nature
and sportsmanship
are out by early light
to check their traps
only to return home
empty-handed
and cushioned
by the morning mist
the quiet of trees and water

Trappers on Return

Under the heavy blue of dawn
our pace back to the house
pushed up from our going out
we step along
strong as deer
and delicately as men
hungry and ignoring
the stings of small twigs
snapping at our faces
our feet imprinting the dew dressed grass

Above us
in dangerous exactitude
the fractal artistry
of tree limbs
black etchings
against the morning light
and off to the side
creek water
reflecting moving silver

Behind us
the dawn mist
erasing itself
in our wake

We are together
empty handed

Dr. Gordon Wilson - How I Remember Him

This is an article in common linear prose I wrote for *The Kentucky Explorer*, a wonderful magazine which often includes folklore columns he wrote years ago.

First this then that
and only in correct order
or go back and do it again

Like playing Mozart
when I was ten

I follow steel railroad tracks
that go to attractive places
but stop at a station
to unload and load
in that order
and move along to the next
always with the knowledge
that I'll run the route again
somehow

Like playing Mozart
when I was ten

Dr. Gordon Wilson - How I Remember Him

The first time I saw Dr. Wilson, that I remember, was the day I walked into Freshman English at the beginning of the fall semester at Western Kentucky State College in 1956. He stopped me, examined me and proceeded to recite the names of my parents and four brothers and three sisters in chronological order and with their full names. I was flabbergasted. And he did this same mental feat with several other new students also. By the end of that first period of class, he knew the full names of each of us and where each was from.

Since I came from Florida, I was looked on as someone from outer space. In those days, when people asked where you were from, they meant what Kentucky county. I enjoyed watching the confusion in that class during the time we had to introduce ourselves when I told them I was from Pinellas County. Dr. Wilson also laughed at that. His laugh was infectious and set everyone into stitches. It was more like an explosion, a loud, nasal "haaaaah" that jarred us.

His memory for everything, as far as I could tell, was instant and rarely fallible - people, places, incidents, tales, expressions, birds, quotations, authors, books, poems, foreign words, rules of spelling, rules of usage, etc., etc., etc. Without doubt, he was the brightest teacher I ever encountered at any school. Some of you know his name from the occasional articles by him in *The Kentucky Explorer*. I suppose a sizable number were taught by him.

One peek at his photo tells you he had intense eyes

(light blue), so intense I don't recall ever seeing him blink, though I am sure he did. He was owlish in facial features and stature, about five feet five inches tall and about half that wide. He was in his late sixties in 1956 with hair that stood straight out from his head - one would imagine that he had just grabbed hold of an electric fence. He always seemed electrified, and he hooted when telling us that his flat top had been in and out of style three times in his lifetime. Remember, flat tops were the rage in the late 1950's. And here we were, freshmen and scared to death, leaping every time he hooted that laugh. He was poking fun of his rotund body, his beaklike nose, and those ears, which were twice the size of ours. I had never heard an old man cackling at his own appearance. What would he do to us if he had such fun laughing at himself? We rolled our eyes at each other in apprehension.

He walked painfully like the tick-tock arm of a metronome, always in a charcoal or black suit and tie with a vest if the weather were not too hot. I never saw him without his gold Phi Beta Kappa key hanging from his jacket. When he talked, usually his fluency was too fast and too interesting for me to keep up. It took a while to figure out that the clacking noises were his "store boughten teeth," he called them, with another hoot-blast. In class, he was vigilant to everything near and far. Some of his colleagues swore he could identify the gender, age, and type of bird by its whistle in a tree one block down College Street, which sloped down the hill below his classroom.

I saw him driving his car a few times. Someone had to tell me who it was because all I could see of him was the top of his head. He drove slowly as if he were at the reins of a horse-drawn wagon.

I took every possible class with Dr. Wilson before he had to retire when he reached the age of seventy at the end of my junior year: both semesters of *Freshman English*, *Survey of American Literature*, *Chaucer*, and the dreaded back-breaking *History and Development of the English Language* (half of which was pure grammar and diagramming). Word around campus was: if you can't do hard work, don't sign up with Dr. Wilson. Small school valedictorians were in for a shock in his class. He tolerated no complacency or laziness. An A grade in his class was a rarity. As I recall, the famous mystery writer, Sue Grafton, earned an A in one of the classes we had with him. I earned five B's with him and felt like they were A+'s.

My first composition - "theme," he called it - came back to me with more red ink on it than my black ink. Those were the days of fountain pens. He kept two, one blue and one red - red with blood, I thought. That theme cost me hours of sweat in revising it - and learning by my numerous mistakes. We wouldn't dare turn in a sentence fragment or a run-on sentence. A misspelled word was a cardinal sin. The rules of agreement, capitalization, and punctuation were rigid and imbedded in stone. His adherence to these rules was manic. No exceptions. In his own writings he wielded the same strictures resulting in, I thought, rigid, mechanical prose. Regardless, I loved what he wrote because his content maintained the human touch, and it was vastly interesting.

A twenty-five pound typewriter was in his office and another one at his home. He pounded out his writings with two fingers at demonic speed and gnashing of his false teeth. When we timidly turned in our final drafts - revised painstakingly - of a theme (along with the outlines and all supporting work and rough drafts), we knew he would not miss a single error. Nor would he fail to acknowledge our successes and growth. After he returned our work, which was at the beginning of the very next class session, we were allowed a short time to assimilate the grade and his red ink. Then, as was his habit, he took everything back up and stored them at his home. At the end of the semester he would burn them all in the big steel barrel behind his home. In this way, there would be no temptation for anyone to cheat or recycle a theme or research paper. He also kept a listing of every topic his pupils researched to insure that no topic was ever duplicated. I wonder how college English teachers handle the cheating problem in this time of personal computers. In fact, the cutting edge of technology in the English Department was a cranky old mimeograph machine and a new ditto machine. Remember those ditto machines? The teacher would hand out a test and the sheet was still slightly moist and mysterious to sniff.

If Dr. Wilson were to proof-read this article, he would certainly reach for his red fountain pen. Writers today have more freedom with Standard English than then. It seems nowadays that fragments and run-on's can enliven prose and promote the author's style. He would call this rationale "pure hooey."

On the lighter side, Dr. Wilson made us howl with laughter at least once every class session. Some of his anecdotes, corny jokes, academic oddities, and antics were pure joy. One time I was walking down a hall in Cherry Hall and he leaped out from behind a door yelling like a ten year old and then collapsing in hoots and snorts of laughter when I jumped at least a foot off the floor screaming like a terrified puppy. One February 14th, he quoted a string of the corniest rhymes ever written. They came out of candy wrappers from before WW I. Two of them were so bad I still remember them and trot them out to my friends on Valentine's Day:

> "My love for you will ever flow
> like water down a tater row."
>
> and
>
> "As sure as vines grow round a stump,
> you are my little sugar lump."

He adored poking fun at deserving people and institutions. I have known no person more skilled at iconoclasm, and he never was guilty of restraint in shattering the images of the pompous, the snide, the puffed-up, the arrogant, the fakers, those who "put on airs," snobs, the reserved egoist, terminally cute cheerleaders, strutting athletes, maidens swooning, Civil War vets marching in a town parade and standing so tall their capes didn't touch anything but the tops of their shoulders, people with awful wigs, people who wore garish jewelry, people who stunk up the place with perfume or cologne, any type of superficiality, and inflated advertisements.

Did I leave any out? To him, nothing was more redundant than last year's beauty queen or last year's star athlete. He actively disliked the basketball coach, who was crude and fractured the English language. Even village idiots were fair game for humorous stereotyping. He used these images and stereotypes to inject humor in our studies. Numerous times I have heard him fire off a diatribe against some nonsense or fad that was sweeping the nation and ask, "Let's give five assorted hoots for (whatever)" followed by five assorted Dr. Wilson hoots with his eyes crossed which left us teary-eyed with laughter. You can only imagine what a field day he had with the writings of Benjamin Franklin or Chaucer's pilgrims. The term "Old Fogy" was used a bit in those days to describe a conservative old relic. When he saw any of us squirming while he was poking fun at some stereotype or institution, he would call us "Young Fogies" and then have a fine fit of hoots. We loved him for helping us laugh at ourselves. I will never forget his description of a humble family at the wake of their no-count, lazy, abusive, drunken father and how they wept, threw themselves into the coffin, and carried on over what a good man he had been and how he was surely sitting at the right hand of God Almighty.

In the Chaucer course, we did not read those ribald tales in modern English. That would be far too easy. We had to translate them from the Middle English of the 1300's which was filled with Old English, Anglo-Saxon, French, and Latin.

When we hit upon a particularly juicy, sex-riddled, nasty part, he would grin and proclaim, "We'll skip the next six lines," which set us to marking places to go back for careful study. I still have that textbook fully marked with notes and underlinings of possible ways to translate words and phrases. I never heard him tell a dirty joke or make crude or salacious comments.

Before the terms "nerd" or "dweeb" insinuated themselves into our media-based vernacular, the term "egg-head" was used to describe a scholarly person, and it was not meant to be a compliment. I was so proud of him when one day he announced, with some heat, "I am proud to be an egg-head! Who would want to be ordinary or stupid?!" He was a proud egg-head who did not drink or smoke either.

Dr. Wilson (born in 1888) came from a tiny village named New Concord which he re-named Fidelity in his writings. It is now long gone and under Kentucky Lake. His father was a country physician. The Westward Migration was still strong when Gordon Wilson was growing up. Wagon trains and families moved through his town on their way West. He recalled for us the people he saw and knew. Like most, they were hard-working people struggling to survive and to make life better for themselves and their families. Since his father was a doctor, it was common for him to see people with a crescent bitten out of an ear, a missing nose, an eye gouged out, crippled limbs, rotten teeth, and early death.

The young Gordon Wilson taught in rural schools for two or three years and then, in 1908 at age twenty, came to what was to become Western. Soon he was teaching Latin and English there and remained until his retirement in 1959. A life-long keeper of facts and figures, he said he taught over 36,000 pupils. Some years he taught every class period every school day - over 400 different pupils at a time - and he wasn't the only teacher doing that. The pay was punishingly inadequate. Western survived very hard times back then.

Eventually he earned his Ph. D. from Indiana University, and he chaired the English Department "On the Hill" for many, many years. When I was at Western, there were only a few teachers with doctorates. Dr. Wilson was the first permanent faculty member who was a product of Western when it was a Normal school - and several others followed. Certainly there were a few other legendary teachers on campus - and a few idiots. Having a doctorate did not insure great teaching. I was awed by the teaching skills of Miss Frances Richards, Miss Margie Helm, and Miss Sybil Stoneciper. Each was profoundly bright and ponderously educated and lacking a doctorate. There is an interesting book by Lowell H. Harrison, *Western Kentucky University*, University Press of Kentucky, 1987, that tells of those days.

I had heard of Dr. Gordon Wilson most of my life. My mother studied with him - she graduated with a degree in English and Latin in 1925. My oldest sister, Betty, also had English classes with him and graduated with a degree in Elementary Education in 1952. I graduated with a degree in English and Latin in 1960. While I was still living at home, Mother and Betty were never shy about relating Dr. Wilson stories to me and about how much they loved and respected him as a teacher. In fact, Dr. Wilson's newspaper columns, "Tidbits of Kentucky Folklore" were the model for Mother's own weekly columns in our little town newspaper - "From My Kitchen Window." My uncle, Herman Lowe, also modeled his columns and letters to the *Park City Daily News* after Dr. Wilson's columns. Mother and Dr. Wilson sent each other packets of their columns from time to time for comparison and encouragement. To me, they are more valuable than gold.

I arrived at Western a late bloomer for academics and barely able to write a coherent sentence or spell ten words in a row correctly. On top of that, I was shy. Those first days were quite a culture shock, but I had no idea that I would ever meet or see the great Dr. Wilson. During the first morning of the first day, we took some sort of placement test, and, boom, I was assigned to Dr. Wilson for English 101a. Freshman English was to be with the man who was revered and loved by my mother and sister, and both of them were excellent students. What would he do to me? To his credit, Dr. Wilson insisted on teaching several beginning English classes to those who scored high enough on the placement test. He could have taught the more interesting classes and passed on highly demanding freshman classes to teachers less experienced. His thinking was that he should bear his part of the burden.

The day I graduated, the man in front of me in line turned to me and said he had never read a book the whole time he was at Western. The woman behind me bragged that she had never been to the library. I felt sorry for them and what they had missed. For four years I had read stacks of books and almost lived in the library - because I had the good fortune to start out as a student of Dr. Gordon Wilson.

He and his wife lived in a small house on Chestnut, which later became a fraternity house (he would have been horrified by this). His wife reminded me of Mrs. Santa Claus, a kind and dear lady. As I recall, their daughter was in journalism, and their son became a professor of chemistry at Western (Dr. Gordon Wilson, Jr.).

Did I tell you his full name was actually Alexander Gordon Wilson? For some reason he avoided that first name and, I'm sure, regretted ever telling me. Every letter or card I sent to him was addressed to Dr. Alexander Gordon Wilson, Sr., a private joke to make him hoot that laugh of his. After he retired, the library was moved to the old gym (Margie Helm Library), and the old library building on top of the hill was re-named Gordon Wilson Hall in his honor.

In addition to his widely circulated articles, "Tidbits of Kentucky Folklore," which are treasures, he wrote two books, *Fidelity Folks* and *Passing Institutions*. Both are utterly charming and scholarly in their accounting of folklore. I gave my copies of them to one of my brightest pupils. Whenever I talked with Dr. Wilson about his writings, he was never kind about the typesetters or editors of them - they would make errors in his perfect text and then print them. In addition, he wrote a double handful of pamphlets equally interesting. To hear Dr. Wilson as a speaker was like listening to a short, banty-legged Joe Creason - each with boy remaining in their faces - both of these Kentucky icons of folklore were charming and hilarious and both easy with words.

Part of being an egg-head professor meant being fair to all. In those early days of desegregation, he was a clear-minded supporter. He had grown up ("growed up" he would hoot in imitation of country pronunciation) with former slaves and their children, and he knew human misery and institutional injustice. His stance was an act of bravery to me. There were some professors at Western who were staunch segregationists and bigots.

While we were sneaking around with novels like *The Catcher in the Rye*, *Tom Jones*, *Lady Chatterly's Lover*, and *Payton Place* in brown paper bags, he let us know that we should read widely if we ever wanted to be well-educated. We discovered in his classes that literature was the best plaything for making fun of people and their customs. Further, if we wanted to be well read, we should read all the works of the best great writers. He had read all of Thackery, Dickens, Shakespeare, Irving, and a few dozen others which stymied us to think about. Does anyone read Thackery - all of him - anymore? We were such young fogies.

Dr. Wilson's studies of folk language in the Mammoth Cave Region (one of the last in Kentucky to receive electricity and radios) is cited in textbooks of American dialects. He was named an honorary citizen of that region. This amazing little man adored listening to people as they talked and then surprising them by identifying what county they came from -

even, in one case, which side of the highway they lived on (near Hopkinsville).

He was an assiduous ornithologist. Country folks seeing him on a bird counting walk referred to him as "that bird man." To accompany him on one of his bird walks was the highest compliment he could offer. One time, he wrote to me, he took a young professor along with him on a bird walk. When they came up to a barbed-wire fence, the scholarly young man hesitated and admitted that he had never climbed over one before. Dr. Wilson was aghast. He placed high value on the ordinary and on living life through experience. In his thinking, a fine scholar could never explain or fully appreciate poetry or other literature or the complications of language by placing academic learning over actual life experiences. For the young man to have a doctorate and not to know how to climb over a barbed wire fence was unforgivable. He wrote, "I never put much store in his scholarship after that."

The study of word histories fascinated him, and, therefore, me. Philology. He surprised us all one day by stating his opinion that the best Webster's dictionary was at least 60% inaccurate because of its guesswork in word histories. That didn't sound much like some of my other English professors who acted as though Merriam-Webster's Dictionary was law. Then he added that it was still the best there is in the United States. Iconoclasm at work!

After I graduated and had begun teaching at Bloomfield High School, during a visit home to Florida my mother handed me a letter he had written to her about me. In those days in the South, sons and daughters rarely heard praise from their parents or siblings. That was considered bragging and, therefore, bad manners. It was some sort of morbid disgrace to be overtly affirming in acknowledging the achievements of a daughter or son. Mother practiced this, as did Dr. Wilson. But it was acceptable to offer compliments to the parents of a student who had done well. Dr. Wilson did that in his letter. He "bragged on me" to my mother. She said nothing, but I still have it tucked among my treasured photos and other papers, a letter with a life like a small animal in my album, and tears well up whenever I read it. By then he knew me better than my family - my strengths and weaknesses, my values and joys, my fears and daring. Could he have known that I modeled myself after him, my brilliant mentor and surrogate parent?

Sometime in 1970, during his eighties, Alexander Gordon Wilson, Sr., Ph. D., died. I had visited him the year before, and he hugged me and cried briefly as old and dearly loved teachers do - as I do now when my special students come to see me. We sat in the swing on his little front porch that evening and talked about life, the war in Vietnam that had killed several of his former pupils, the excitement of teaching in rural schools, and the discouraging pay teachers earned. We cackled about the continuing human comedy about us. And, underneath our quiet words there was another dimension of thought. I felt the strength which he had passed on to me and to countless others, the strength to look honestly into the future and to honor the past with knowledge, experience, reverence, and a hoot or two.

Some Thoughts About Our Music Teacher

I wrote this article in common linear prose for the Dunedin Historical Society to place in their archives. Miss Helene Goss taught generations of people in Dunedin. This included all eight of the Boyd children. With her I learned to poo-poo any thoughts that a person was born with a "talent" for musicianship. There was no doubt that skill in music required commitment, hard practice, and discipline. Even Mozart practiced. Throughout those years as her pupil, I discovered so much about music in my own life, and it has made all the difference.

Some Thoughts About Our Music Teacher

Miss Helene Goss was born in 1879, either in Switzerland or Germany, I have never been certain. Her family was wealthy - ribbon manufacturing. She once showed me a photo of her childhood home somewhere in the North East where they lived before an economic depression in the late 19th century - a plantation-like mansion with pillars and a great lawn. She had studied piano and violin (and other strings) in Europe and later at Julliard in New York. Miss Goss also studied violin with the great violinist and teacher, Leopold Auer. To him Tchaikovsky dedicated his violin concerto, which he famously refused saying it was unplayable in its original form.

After that economic depression, she and her brothers moved to Tampa where Miss Goss played principal violin in the Tampa Philharmonic. One of her brothers, I recall, began work with customs at the port there. Eventually she and Albert, another brother, relocated to Dunedin where she began teaching piano and violin and he set up a clock/watch repair business in the octagonal house on Scotland Street. Miss Goss remained unmarried and lived directly behind Albert's home in a very small cottage. Albert and his wife had several children - one son flew planes from the landing strip north of Dunedin. Miss Goss often mentioned a niece, Maybeth (Marybeth), who cared for her in Alabama during her last years.

During the move to Florida, Miss Goss and her family managed to keep their ancient string instruments along with large leather-bound copies of music - and probably more. Her violin was over two hundred years old when I saw it in the 1950's. The curved head piece was shaped like a ram's head and had ruby eyes. It had a tone that was astonishing to my ears and to my touch. In a letter to me later, she mentioned selling the instruments.

Albert's house was fascinating. He seemed ancient to me when I was a boy. To take a watch to him for repair was a trip into another world. On entering the octagonal house, I was surrounded by dozens of clocks. All shapes and sizes, regular alarm clocks, grandfather clocks, art pieces, and music boxes, each one alive and clicking and clacking and sounding at the same time. There was one in particular that I vividly remember - a bronze statue of Mercury, the size of a four year old maybe. He was in flight holding out an orb of the earth in his outstretched hand. A pendulum swinging back and forth hung below the orb which served as the clock's face with its minute and hour hands. Mr. Goss sat at a table on which were tiny watch parts along with small paper packets of more parts. Each watch and clock was tagged with the owner's name and the date it was brought to him. He wore a series of magnifying lenses attached to the front of his regular glasses. I remember hearing Mrs. Goss in the back of the house, but I don't recall ever seeing her.

Miss Goss had a car - a two seater dark blue coupe, a relic from the early 1920's, that she rarely drove and only with great dignity and care. Ordinarily she walked the short distance to town for her shopping. I was scandalized when she mentioned to me that she enjoyed drinking a single beer on weekends. At that time, I knew no-one who drank alcohol. From time to time she would also dye her hair a reddish black, though a small circular crown at the top of her head was bald.

Her little cottage - studio, she called it - included one small darkened room for teaching her lessons. It had an old upright piano that had been a player piano earlier in its life, with rigid, thick keys covered with yellowing ivory. She sat in an upright chair at the right of the piano armed with pencils and the pupil's lesson book (one of those Blue Book composition booklets with the multiplication matrix on the back cover) on her lap and her pet dog under her chair. There was a lamp near two stuffed chairs at the back of the room. On the piano was a lamp arching out over the music. To the left of the piano was a thick, carved piece of furniture that held her family's bound tomes of music and her stringed instruments.

The east side of her cottage was a former porch, which was screened-in from midway up to the low roof. This was where she slept except on those rare, very cold nights when she went to Albert's house. The screens had thick shades, which she pulled down for privacy.

Behind the piano's wall was a tiny room containing her kitchen and bath. A path led from it to the octagonal house where she usually ate. Also, I recall, she cooked cabbage for herself on Saturdays and stunk up the neighborhood. Arching over her cottage was a huge oak tree laden with Spanish moss. The last time I walked past the octagonal house, Miss Goss's cottage was gone, a flat extension of the lawn obliterating any evidence of her home or the music that came from it for so many years.

She was devoted to her series of dogs, usually strays. The one that survived my years of lessons was proficient in farting. At least I hope it was the dog.

Of the Boyds, we all took piano lessons from Miss Goss. Richard and I also studied violin with her. I later played in various symphonies in Louisville and Bowling Green and loved our concerts, playing many of the greatest symphonic works and a few operas. Several of my siblings became proficient on the piano. I especially loved playing it, though I hated solo piano concert work and recitals. I later learned to play pipe organs in churches and did for a number of years - all with respect to my beloved Miss Goss.

I began piano in the second grade. John Thompson, Book I, the same one the older four had used their first years. That initial lesson terrified me because Jayne, my sister, had told me that Miss Goss had a lampshade of human skin and a mummy in her closet. That was at the end of WWII, and word was that Miss Goss was German. Images of the war from newsreels flickered vividly in my mind. I had seen "The Mummy's Ghost" at the Capitol Theater in Clearwater, a scary movie, which sent me hiding under the seat.

When I dutifully appeared at Miss Goss's side door, I knocked, her dog barked, and the screen door opened. I looked straight ahead, terrified, and encountered Miss Goss's pale white legs with her stocking rolled down around her ankles like doughnuts, and I peed in my pants in horror fully expecting the mummy to lurch out and grab me. She sent me home and told me to come back later. When I did, she inspected my hands and fingernails and admonished me to trim my nails and keep them clean. She explained the keyboard, the white keys and black, the combinations of black keys in twos and threes. Then she had me point to my belly button. I did. She pushed down on middle C and said that when I sit at the piano always align my navel to middle C. I still do that.

My lessons continued until the fifth grade when I decided playing the piano was not manly. However, I returned in the seventh grade, I think it was - and zoomed along from then on. Scales and arpeggios, etudes, Czerny, Mozart, Beethoven, Haydn, and others. The fundamentals. Music from the Classical Era. Then came the music of the Romantic Era. All that Chopin. And later, the Twentieth Century Era and its challenging gymnastics for my hands. I must have driven my mother crazy with my practice, which I loved. It was when I was introduced to J. S. Bach that I entered another, loftier world similar to math, which I also loved.

Piano became my emotional safe place. However, it

was private to me except when I was required to perform during the dreaded annual recitals. I still break out in a sweat when I smell gardenias - which the girls often wore to those recitals. My father, non-musician that he was, never missed an opportunity to diminish any pride I might have felt after my performance by announcing to me, "I heard your mistake." Even Miss Goss was not one to brag or emote about a performance. For my ninth grade recital piece, I played seventeen pages of the original Grieg Concerto from memory, and at my next lesson she slightly smiled and told me her brother thought I had played it brilliantly. Praise by proximity, I suppose.

Sometime during high school, it became apparent to me that the music I loved was not the music of my peers. Elvis had appeared on the scene by then. Hank Williams, Frank Sinatra, and Doris Day were popular icons. I asked Miss Goss, "Do you like ordinary music? You know. Like on the radio. Be-bop. Ballads. Crooning?"

She gave me an understanding look and said, "Most people are illiterate about music. Serious music, that is. If they are caught up in popular music and reject serious music, that is all right with me. I understand. I look at it just like many other things. Most people back away from the unfamiliar. On occasion, I hear a tune on the radio that is quite appealing. But when I compare popular music to the great music of the world, I choose the great music." So do I. So do I.

I'm not sure when Miss Goss died. The last letter I received from her was in 1968. I had written to her to tell her how much she had filled my life. All those lessons - many at night. The thrill I had in exploring new music and old with her as my teacher - and for decades after I left Dunedin. The joy of feeling music pour out of my hands. She had nurtured a hollow place in me and filled it with music. And for so very many others, too. The memory of Miss Helene Goss remains warm in my heart.

The Fourth of July, 2011

This is also an article written somewhat in Virginia Woolf's style which employs long sentences that sprout and grow but make good sense. I wrote it for the members of my biological family, to share with them the comforts and joys I have in being a surrogate member of the Simpson family of Bloomfield, KY.

The Fourth of July, 2011

Forgive my sins for writing this while violating all manner of those dire warnings I taught in English composition classes (which do not bother me in the least at this advanced age), but I want to share the beauty of yesterday's Independence Day at the Simpson Farm - so dear to my heart - with my own far flung relatives.

I lived there for many years, and I remain a member of them, of their three living generations, most of them present this one time of year, kinfolks and friends coming in from close by and a few from far away. I am now one of their elders, walking slower, greeting her on the porch and then him over there next to the rock wall where the coal pile had been, sometimes with a handshake or even a hug, and watching the newest crop of newborns being passed around: finding it touching to see one infant being carefully held by a young man, slim and with strong arms, and another bundled and watched over by its mother, while a little girl, barely eight, cuddles another lump of fat-baby with its amazing eyes and puckered mouth, my companion elders and I cooing and damp-eyed at what our beloved Mrs. Simpson, the matriarch now long gone, would have remarked to all of us about each of this new brood four generations down from her, and I hear her laughter echoing all around this place, this farmhouse as we, the new elders, sit under the trees behind the back kitchen door, not far from the old meat house and, farther on, the revered outhouse which someone has added new flat boards to, covering over the missing slats through which each of us looked out at the trees and garden years ago as we sat; however, I helped Jim add a bathroom to the house years ago which the elementary-aged kids ignore in favor of the outhouse and its fascination. (Now that was a Virginia Woolf sentence!)

In front of us, in front of the line-up of elders and new mothers on rows of fold-up chairs under the shade of the trees, is The Great Softball Game. The field has a gentle slope up to the tobacco barn, which is no longer in use as such but is still handsome, grayer, ragged, and its front door open and side vents blown off - one edge is the out-of-bounds for left field. There are at least one hundred kinfolk and a stray number of friends here, and about half are young, less than eighteen - about half of those are children in motion and alerted not to step in the horseshit or cow patties - some successfully heeding those cautions - many barefoot and connected by their feet to the grass, the weeds, the cool green and freedom of this farmland - little groups of girls with loose hair and arms up and surfing and their fingers feeling the air, little boys racing around each other and taking time to edge up close to the big boys, studying them with those looks of want in their eyes, silent pleads of wishing to hold the bat and be like them, like these bigger ones without shirts, teenagers with long legs and flashing eyes towering above them. I am touched by how the big boys do notice the little ones and do nurture them, leaning down to show how to hold the bat, how to take the batter's stance, telling them when to run and slide.

The game is really in two parts. The major part is for the bigger ones to play with semi-seriousness, for them to whack that ball, a solid clink metallic sound that causes the horses on the side of this field to lift their heads in inquiry, and ah's and ooh's rise up from the elders' row as the ball arcs over the outfield and down to the edge of the creek beneath the brush there.

The other part is a smoothly injected interlude when three or four little folks are given a time at bat, and we watch as, usually, one after the other makes it across home plate -

but not always. Some strike out. Occasionally one is put out on second or third or even crossing home. There is a collective commitment among the older players about teaching success and failure and fun to this next generation of the family. A rite of passage, it seems to me.

A word about the Fourth of July Softball Game. With all these younger people wanting to play ball, I am comfortably amused at the outfield during each inning because sometimes there are as many as twenty people, little and big, out there - and there is one big boy who goes to right field who is followed, like a line of ducklings, by six little ones who stay close to him, and he encourages them and talks sports with them, and they absolutely love him, their eyes looking upward to his face. Those big guys! I note that they have mastered their struts and know the game and are in deep competition with each other - but not up to the point of anger, easily awarding to each other little pats and high fives and the umpteen enactments of body language that say, "We are playing a game on Independence Day at the farm and the little guys love us and are waiting to be us so keep it cool - still, I have to assert my masculinity and strength."

Now a few more words about the little ones when the time comes for three or four to bat one after the other. A group of them is permitted to play through every three or four innings. This is my favorite part of the game. The pitcher, an elder who is a wise sports judge and player, steps forward, closer to the little batter who has a big-boy volunteer coach, his role model on whom an affectionate bond is firmly fixed. These little ones are fearless. Each one takes a stance and addresses home plate, which is a paper dinner plate, tapping it with the bat, takes some show-off swings, and maybe even spits, something he has observed and practiced throughout the waiting period, and then lifts his eyes calling out to the pitcher, challenging without words, "Give me your best shot." The ball is lobbed gently. Maybe several times. We wait through a wild strike or two, through several balls high in the air, and then, "clink," the metal concussion, and the ball bounces around the infield beneath the feet of three or four guys who intentionally kick and drop and fumble it long enough for the batter, with invisibly fast legs, races to first base, the first baseman stretching out for show as if to catch a mighty hurl from third base, the first base coach dancing about to bring the boy safely in - which happens, of course. The boy (now be fair - sometimes it's a little girl with long hair streaming behind her and equal in all ways to those little boys, except in their acquired art of spitting - for now, at least) over-runs the base and happily dances back the same as he has watched the big boys do, though with a solemn face modestly deflecting the cheers from the elders and the mommas under the trees - mommas who are so proud and attached to the little ones and to the bigger nurturing ones, those idols who offer the base hitter a hand to slap and a touch on the shoulder along with a quick look of "You did ok." I am touched and impressed by the gentleness of this enacting. Every step along the way the process is without rancor or putdowns or sarcasm. A continuation of one generation into the next. And I realize that most of these big boys went through this a few years back, idolizing the earlier generation of big boys who are now the grown men. This is family. This is family at play, relaxed and connected this one time each year. And I am in awe of it and a part of it.

After nine innings, the pitcher announces, "It's time to eat" - to line up for a covered dish extravaganza set out on the side porch, on tables. He firmly states: "The oldest people eat first and youngest eat last." What? Children eat last? This is unheard of among the little ones, and they keep looking up at the big ones to see if this is some sort of joke because, "We always eat first at home!!!" - but not here where the old rules of eating are observed. Can you imagine their impatience amid such diminishment and dismissal, the anxiety for little ones to watch as the old, shaky-handed ones take forever at the head of the line? There are two or three people fanning with paper plates to keep the flies away, and on the tables are cheese laden dishes and country green beans with ham-hocks and plates of fried chicken, of course, and rolls and an entire table devoted to desserts, most of them homemade. But - uh-oh! - there is a pause before the oldest lady begins to pick and shake her way over the dishes, when the soft-ball pitcher, a military veteran, requires all to bow their heads in prayer and afterwards everyone is to join in singing the National Anthem, which many do and others, embarrassed at not knowing the words and in fear of "looking like a darn fool next to my favorite cousin or my mother-in-law," lip-sync and croak out a tone or two here and there. At its ending, almost everyone thinks or says, "Aren't we supposed to shout 'Play ball!' now?", and they smile at each other apologetically. Then the polite filling of plates begins. Here and there one person is carrying two plates, the second for a beloved one who has trouble walking or who is nursing. And around the edges of the crowd are the dear ones who have set out the food and are the guardians of the tables, who are smiling and sticking an arm in here and there to remove an empty dish or add more green beans or encourage a little one to "try some of this."

After the food, the second softball game begins. This time the little ones are more demanding about their turns, and the big ones don't hold back hitting the ball with all their strength. Yet, there is no rancor, not a single cuss word or put-down. I hear friendly comments, encouragements that don't morph into sarcasm. The rooters behind the fence with me remain loyal fans, though they sometimes have to be told to look up at some important play because they are busy with storytelling or looking at camera pictures on those new-fangled cell-phones and digital cameras, and visiting with each other, catching up on sicknesses, the kids, work, church, neighbors, the recession, books, schooling, clothes, babies, and on and on.

After the second softball game, there is a long lull which is needed and anticipated - until it is dark enough for The Fireworks. I like this time because it's open for us, for the elders to visit, often looking straight ahead as we indulge ourselves in gentle and wry teasing, usually oblique as is often the case in the rural areas, an art we have perfected, while we softly call up our own collective moral and legal departures and histories - the next generation listening in and adding this lore to their family memories. And it is a time, also, when the little ones really go at it - running, doing the fire-fly thing, exploring, perching close to the bigger ones to soak up their smells and wisdom, being picked up and rolled around on big shoulders and squeezed and plunked back down, little ones exploring farther and farther away yet in sight of Momma or adored Grammaw or Pea-Paw, and then coming back seeking assurance and a touch of two, maybe even a brief cuddle in the arm-warmth there. I watch a girl carefully touching a fishing pole, getting the feel of it in her fingers. She is quiet and pensive. And a little boy is pulling in the evening country air through his nose and is wide-eyed at the hay smells, planning to remember them later. There is one boy, though, whom I have observed throughout most of this day. Reed thin like his grand-daddy fifty years before on this same occasion and here at the farm. Look-alikes. He has been in motion all day, but it is not aimless. It is purposeful and lightning fast, darting from place to place, into everything. What amazes me is watching his hands and feet. They seem to have lives of their own, disconnected from the rest of him. Emotive. Spontaneous. Supplemental to his actions, ancillary and detached. Did I ever romp around and be that spontaneous? No. He never seems to tire. And down the row of us, sits Grand-daddy, also watching the boy. He nods and smiles. I am a sap for little children, too - their spontaneity and intelligence and energy. Playful as young otters. I know each child will not remember being put to bed tonight.

I am a watcher. Always. It is my vicarious way, I suppose. Yet I am a part of all this. Free to breathe in and out without a single hint, here in this place, of score-keeping or shaming or put-downs. Not in this family. I am included and I include myself with easy face and easy love here, among my surrogate family.

Fat Ass

In this age of rampant obesity, I just couldn't omit a story about being fat, which I have struggled with for decades. For years I attended Overeaters Anonymous - a men's group. We had some heartfelt sessions sharing our skirmishes with food. The rationales listed here came from our meetings.

Fat Ass

Now then, let's see. You want to know why I let myself get so fat? And why I am so flippant about it? So self-centered and stand-offish? Short answer: I eat too much and don't exercise enough. Of course I know that. Doesn't help a bit. Other people, at least the sleek, athletic, slender ones like you, appear to be mostly outside of themselves and using people as their drugs of choice. People - and not food. But you and those other real people, the beautiful and handsome ones, tear through intimacies so easily. Not me. I'm more sensitive. I watch you folks and wonder. Pretty much like watching horses in a field. The ways they effortlessly herd with each other and whisper and nod and sometimes romp up the hill and back and then waller in the dust. Always needing each other. Never having problems with body image. Well, dammit, I'm not like that. I don't need people. I NEED food, not you real people.

I went to see my primary care physician, and she didn't mince words as she flipped through my chart. Reading up-side-down, I locked in on the first sentence at the top, the very top of my summary. "Pt 46 yr old <u>obese</u> cau. male..." That word "obese" was underscored. She ran her finger down my blood work report and paused at triglycerides, both cholesterols, and blood sugar giving me a look and a brief commentary about each. Yeah, yeah. Same ole, same ole from her. She's not fat.

What did I think about her report? Guilt. Shame. Full of GUILT AND SHAME!! Thanks, Doc. I really needed that. And all I could think about was what I would have for a snack before supper when I got back home.

And now I am at the park. On the walking track. With people. All sorts of them. The beautiful and the ugly. The ordinary and the lame. Even a few "fatty fatty two by four, can't get through the bathroom door." Like me.

So, while I'm strolling along, I'll force myself to be honest about my food. About my eating behaviors. What are the countable and visible behaviors involving my food intake? I have to be honest now - for this inventory. Maybe this is what I've been in denial about, my warped and tangled thinking as I shove down food and gobble up the calories.

FIFTEEN RATIONALES FOR OVEREATING

The top reason that popped out first: I live with a little voice in my head that tells me, "You will starve if you don't eat - you must eat until you're stuffed." Can't have that. I always clean my plate. "Oh, what a good boy! You ate every bite! It's a sin to waste food. Think of all the starving children in Africa."

And further, I guard my food. Did that way back sitting next to my brothers and my classmates. Anyone might sneak up and grab my chicken leg or, horrors, my dessert. Even today, I always keep a clear space around me as I eat. And I watch everyone. Never entirely close my eyes during the blessing and stay as vigilant as a dog with a fresh bone.

As I bring a forkful of food to my mouth, I stop half way, take a good look, bring it to my face, and then lunge at it chewing with my mouth partly open. This way it seems to allow me more forkfuls and more food to keep me from starving.

If two cookies stick together, the second one is free and doesn't count. Same for other food items. If I dish up a serving from a casserole or a delicious vegetable and it amounts to two or more ordinary servings, pay no attention and glop it onto my plate. Counts as one serving.

Any food I find lying around, like a bag of unopened Cheetos, I grab it. Crunch away. It doesn't count as food.

Afterwards I lick my orange fingers clean. No evidence then.

Any food that comes to me as a gift is calorie free and doesn't count. Mustn't hurt the feelings of the giver.

When attending weddings, pot-lucks, funerals, picnics, receptions, or any other time when everyone is invited to graze and load up, I load up again and again. Yummmm! None of it counts as caloric intake.

There are times in life when stealing food might become a possibility. I have to admit to doing this a few times. Even when I had money in my pocket. Pilfered food is free of calories. And, by gum, it does taste better.

Clearing the table after a meal, usually there is a dab or two of food in each of the serving dishes. I would never, NEVER toss food out. I scrape it into my mouth quietly so that no one can see or hear. This is mandatory for crumbs of cakes, pies, and meat scraps. "Finger food," I call it. Leftovers just clutter up the refrigerator, and I don't have pigs to slop.

Holiday foods (Christmas, Halloween, Easter, etc.) provide goodies that are traditional and therefore, free. No calories at all need to be counted. "I'll have another glass of egg custard, please."

This one may require reconsideration, but if visiting a friend in the hospital, it is an act of friendship to snack on whatever has been left on the tray. Then the patient gets credit for feeling better with an improved appetite. "You gonna eat the rest of the meat loaf?"

There will be occasions when I am invited out to a restaurant, but I have just stuffed myself while raiding the refrigerator. Should I demurely decline or go? By all means, grab coat, go, and eat heartily. Do not disappoint host by nibbling. Everyone enjoys eating with a man who has a big appetite.

Girl Scout Cookies never count as food. Stuff them down, especially those chocolate mints. It's for a WORTHY CAUSE. Thus, no calorie counting is needed.

Then, there's that old process of making myself eat one item, say Reece's Cups, until I can't look at another one. To "burn out" on them, as they say. Never has worked for me. I still love them.

And, there's that trick of the mind: if I admit that I'm a compulsive overeater, then I'm not in denial. "Damn right I'm a fat ass overeater. Watch me drop these wedges of pizza in my mouth and laugh at the same time. Oh, what a jolly man am I! But, don't you see? I can't help it. I have a big build and a glandular problem on top of it. And my metabolism..."

I suppose that covers most of it, about my eating behaviors and thinking. I could go all psychological and detail my childhood abuses and the unjust spankings from my father or the ways bullies tortured me every chance they got. But you would just sit there all slender and beautiful and smirk at me.

An Afterword

It's the eyes and soft hands of children
isn't it
they trust in reality
testing it
then they toy and play with it
turn it about
give color to it and mold it
maybe run from it
but they have it in there
behind their eyes
forever